W9-CHQ-804

HOW ANIMALS MATE

SEWANEE WRITERS' SERIES

Wyatt Prunty: General Editor

Readers: John Casey, Alice McDermott, Francine Prose

HOW ANIMALS MATE

STORIES BY

DANIEL MUELLER

SEWANEE WRITERS' SERIES / THE OVERLOOK PRESS

SEWANEE WRITERS' SERIES/THE OVERLOOK PRESS
First published in the United States in 1999 by
The Overlook Press, Peter Mayer Publishers, Inc.
Lewis Hollow Road
Woodstock, New York 12498
editorial offices:
386 West Broadway
New York, NY 12498

Stratford Road
London W8

Copyright © 1999 by Daniel Mueller

All Rights Reserved. No part of this publication may be
reproduced or transmitted in any form or by any means, electronic
or mechanical, including photocopy, recording, or any information
storage and retrieval system now known or to be invented without
permission in writing from the publisher, except by a reviewer who
wishes to quote brief passages in connection with a review written
for inclusion in a magazine, newspaper, or broadcast.

Library of Congress Cataloguing-in-Publication Data

Mueller, Daniel.
How animals mate / Daniel Mueller.
p.   cm.
1. United States—Social life and customs—20th century—Fiction.
I. Title.
PS3563.U3448H69   1999   813'.54—dc21   98-31823

Book Design Yellowstone Ltd. and Bernard Schleifer
Manufactured in the United States of America

ISBN 0-87951-925-8
First Edition
1 3 5 7 9 8 6 4 2

ACKNOWLEDGMENTS

Some of the stories in this collection have appeared elsewhere, in slightly different form: "Torturing Creatures at Night," in *The Crescent Review*; "How Animals Mate," in *The Mississippi Review*; "The Night My Brother Worked the Header," in *Playboy*; "Ice Breaking," in *Elvis in Oz: New Stories and Poems from the Hollins Creative Writing Program*; "Zero," in *Story*; "P.M.R.C.," in *Timbuktu* and *Henfield Prize Stories*.

The author is grateful to Hollins College, the University of Virginia, the University of Iowa Writers' Workshop, the Fine Arts Work Center in Provincetown, the Henfield Foundation, the Massachusetts Cultural Council, the Market Street Wine Shop in Charlottesville, and the National Endowment for the Arts for support during the writing of this book. Thanks are also due everyone who responded critically to the stories in this collection but especially Amy Rosano, Bernardine Connelly, Tom Coash, the late John Hersey, the late Veronica Geng, Alice Turner, John Casey, Molly Turner, Ted Corcoran, Lois Rosenthal, Karen McElmurray, Pam Mandell, Kurt Mueller, Suzy Chamandy, Fred Leebron, Henry Dunow, Jennifer Carlson, Sharon Bandy, and Bob Jones.

Special thanks are due my sister Karen.

For Amy,
and my parents

Contents

By night on my bed I sought
him whom my soul loveth:
I sought him, but I found him not.

—*Song of Solomon* 3:1

HOW ANIMALS MATE

HOW ANIMALS MATE

AT FIFTEEN I WAS A PEEPING TOM FOR A SHORT TIME. MY family had just moved to Minneapolis from Islet, a town on the north shore of Lake Superior seven minutes by bicycle from the Canadian border, and I fell in with the wrong kids, although they were the only kids on the block anywhere near my age, and I wasn't old enough to drive to the neighborhoods of other less perverted kids. Brad Pedroncelli, whom everyone called Pedro, lived with his depressed mother and was only rarely visited by his estranged father, who drove a cherry-red Lamberghini with flip-up doors until the police arrested him for selling stock in a racecar part manufacturing firm that did not exist. Mark Guttenoff, who went by his last name, had two brothers and a sister who were nearly as old as my parents and had all left home before Guttenoff was born. His mother and father were only waiting for him to graduate from high school to move to Scottsdale, Arizona, where they wouldn't have to worry about the drug delivery girl getting snowed-in at the pharmacy. OB was the name Gene O'Brien went by, and he was perhaps the sickest of the three. His mother had moved to

Hollywood to open a gallery of erotic art, and his father, whose occupation no one quite knew, left him alone for weeks on end in a geodesic dome filled with pink plastic *objets d'art* and shelf upon white shelf of pornographic magazines and video cassettes.

Across the street from my house, in a yellow split-level with sliding glass doors for windows and cedar-shingle awnings that flared out from the first and second stories like pagoda roofs, lived Tammy Fitzsimmon, a tall, thin, beautiful girl with features sharp as scalpel blades. Connie was Tammy's mother's name, and she opened all the shutters and blinds in the house, or none, depending on her mood. She also spread a thick layer of sunflower seeds over the front and back lawns to attract Canadian geese, which that summer and fall sometimes numbered a hundred.

Tammy was retaking twelfth grade, or so someone mumbled when she appeared in Accelerated Human Physiology on the first day of school and sat down beside me at the last available desk. Before then I had only seen her getting into a black Rambler that rattled away leaving exhaust and dust roiling above the groomed lawns at our end of Braemar Court, a drive that entwined the houses on it into a bracelet of charms, each different and full of promise. Up close, I saw how her black locks tried to conceal the hoop of a silver earring, how in the serpentine V of her leather jacket, a red blouse with gold paisleys rose and fell, how her legs issued from her skirt like a slipknot in a slack rope.

Mr. Sorenson began the class by sketching a measly valentine on the blackboard. He bisected it from the droop at the top to the point at the bottom and labeled it THE UTERUS. Then he told the class how on such-and-such day at some ungodly hour of the morning my father had delivered his daughter, Elizabeth Howard Lynn, by Caesarean section. Mr. Sorenson, who also coached varsity hockey, explained how Julius Caesar had been delivered by means of a knife, then asked the class to give me, Rich Reville, a round of applause for being the son of so gifted a physician. As kids clapped and whistled, Tammy Fitzsimmon crossed her arms and sighed, and I thought I'd never seen a person look so bored.

That night I told myself I would win Tammy's heart. If she had appeared uninterested, then so would I, and she would see we were alike and meant for each other. But in the days that followed neither she nor her heart were there to win. After two weeks of calling her name, Mr. Sorenson dropped her from the roll, and my only reminder that she had ever been in class at all became a single vacant desk. Mr. Sorenson had no seating chart, and so each day when the last student took a seat I would notice which desk her absence occupied.

NOW OB, PEDRO, AND GUTTENOFF DID NOT STEAL BOOZE from their parents' liquor cabinets, destroy public property, use or distribute illegal drugs as I would with my teammates on the varsity hockey squad. OB and Guttenoff sang in the concert choir and performed Gilbert and Sullivan duets with girls who wanted nothing to do with them outside the show. Pedro wrestled at 155 pounds and even went to the state tournament in Saint Paul where he was pinned three times in under three minutes—yet he was just as courteous and inquiring as the other two were when they came by to get me for a chilly autumn evening of hardcore adult entertainment and voyeurism. "How are you tonight, Dr. and Mrs. Reville?" OB would ask, the three of them standing in the kitchen my mother had decorated with curtains of frilly blue lace and Hummel-Goebel plates my father gave to her every Christmas.

The plates, with the year of their minting printed below each in slender Arabesque numerals, showed a wide-eyed boy and girl engaged in different domestic tasks, from ironing and folding laundry to weeding the garden. As much as my mother hated those plates, she hung them on the wall anyway—for form's sake.

If we weren't through with supper, my father would make my friends laugh with stories about growing up in the dairy lands of central Wisconsin, about tying fishing line to Mrs. Pym's window screen and plucking eerie high-pitched notes from the alley behind her house. Or about yanking the cords on window-rattlers, notched wooden spools pierced through the center with masonry nails. Or about tipping over sleeping Herefords and Guernseys. Sometimes they came over when my father was on the phone with a patient, and my mother would rescue me by asking them questions about their families, questions which they answered as smoothly as mafiosi charming a jury. "My mother has ladies over for cards," Pedro told her once, by which he meant his mother hallucinated the hands as well as the players holding them. "My parents like to go on walks," Guttenoff offered, by which he meant from time to time inside the house. These questions and others, they answered as my father inquired after the color of a patient's urine or the number of days her menstruations had contained pus or whether she could meet him at his office in the morning with a specimen—his voice so professional and kind that often the meanings of his words would not register until after he hung up the receiver, and then I'd doubt I heard them correctly.

One evening when my father was talking to a patient, OB told my mother his father was a filmmaker, and she asked him what films he had made.

"I'll be frank with you, Mrs. Reville," he replied, "people are always asking me that, and I get a little tired of answering because no one's ever heard of any of them."

"Are they documentaries?" my mother asked.

"Yes, they are," he said. "Wildlife documentaries. How animals mate. That sort of thing."

"I see," she said. "Have any been on television?"

OB laughed. "No, never."

"Well I'd like to see one," my mother said.

"No you wouldn't," OB said. "They're so explicit they're boring. Besides, once you've seen one you've seen them all."

Often I would tell my mother I was spending the night at OB's, and she would ask why we four never spent the night at my house, and I would tell her it was because the O'Briens owned a wide-screen TV, a Betamax video player, and a library of feature films on cassette. If my father were off the phone, he would call to us through the bay window, "Don't do anything I wouldn't do!" and OB would holler back, "Don't worry, Dr. Reville!" and I would go with my new friends to a geodesic dome which sat like a wigwam on top of a wooded hill overlooking the strip of parkland behind our houses and, beyond, the fairways and greens of the Braemar Hills Country Club. Sometimes deer would stare at us as we climbed the gravel driveway—fat, corn-fed creatures that barely resembled the white-tailed flashes I'd seen through the jack pines and water birches of the Nett Lake Indian Reservation, not far from Islet, where they were hunted year-round.

OB was always a perfect host because his father stocked the refrigerator only with foods he knew OB liked. Sirloin steaks. Wax-covered specialty cheeses from Holland and France. Perrier sparkling water, which had only just been made available in supermarkets with gourmet food sections. Inside the house everything was white except the art, which was as pink as erasers. "It's erotic," OB explained, though to me it looked more like stalagmites than anything we saw blown up by a factor of ten on a screen I had taken for a partition until OB turned it on. On a coffee table would rest a basket of water crackers, finger-sized pieces of toast, and a platter of *foie gras*. Or perhaps a tulip of caviar and onion canapés, or boiled Alaskan king crab, a bowl of melted butter, and four pairs of pliers. When we had closed the blinds, OB would ask one of us to choose a cassette, which I thought diplomatic of him until I understood he was simply hoping we'd choose something he never had before. Often one of us would have a tape case open, ready to insert the cassette, when OB would tell us he'd seen it already. Then we would choose another, to which he might respond, "I haven't seen that one in about four years," and we would put that tape in.

We always started the videos at the normal speed. Then OB, lying in his father's over-stuffed recliner, the remote control a scepter in his fist, would begin fast-forwarding through the few moments of foreplay and even fewer moments of dialogue. I resented this until I discovered that the sets, situations, acting, props—everything that made a violent R-rated movie believable and good—were distracting and false compared with the close-ups of enmeshed body parts, which looked more like alien life-forms feeding on themselves than anything I imagined two, three, or four consenting adults could accomplish, but which were as real as the tattoos and pieces of jewelry I could see through the knotted limbs and tufts of seaweed-like hair. And so they seemed to me more real than anything I'd witnessed in my fifteen years on the planet.

By nine-thirty or ten, when we had scanned a dozen films and on the coffee table lay the strips of cheese wax, crab leg shells, and bits of liver and fat too identifiable to put in our mouths, we would leave OB's geodesic dome searching for confirmation of what we had seen on the screen. In theory this involved creeping up to the windows of people whom OB, Pedro, and Guttenoff knew and peering in at them as they engaged in sex. But in our neighborhood most people's bedrooms were on the second and third floors, and so the chances of seeing anything like what we *had* seen were diminished by too-high sills or, if we were on a slope or in trees, by curtains, blinds, and darkness. We saw Mr. Desmond, who jetted about the continent installing International Business Machines, kiss his wife Dorea close to her mouth after she poured him a flute of French champagne and presented him a dinner of pheasant under glass. We saw Mrs. MacGibbon, by far the most attractive divorcee on the block, vacuum her living room in a one-piece swimsuit. We saw Mr. Lilligrand, by far the *least* attractive divorcee on the block, consume a bottle of Pabst. And so, as we walked back through the lit cones from streetlamps, Guttenoff would make jokes about how the human race was being perpetuated solely by porn stars.

Often we got back before one o'clock, slammed any old cassette into the deck, and as we fell asleep to the claps of converging bodies, I would find myself on a train car pulled by an engine of bones. One night when I had made up my mind to leave my perverted friends as soon as varsity hockey practice began and to make new friends whose homes I would hike to, however far, Guttenoff said, "Maybe Tammy Fitzsimmon is palucking her boyfriend."

"We looked in on her before," I said, "and never saw anything."

"She wasn't home before," OB said.

"Tonight will be different," Guttenoff said and pointed at

the moon, which hung like a golfball over the bedraggled tops of the elms.

"The moon's as white as spunk," Pedro said proudly.

"What do you say, Reville?" OB asked.

"Sure," I said.

So we cut up between the Kuphals' Dutch colonial and the Goodes' two-story ranch, leaves crunching under our sneakers as the Warners' spitz barked and came crashing across their unraked yard. "Don't get excited, Hoffman," Pedro told the snarling dog, which bared its fangs at him behind the chain links.

Gnarled fingers of light clutched at us through the Kuphals' willow trees as we crept along the edge of the fence. Then their sliding glass door grated on its runner. Falling to our stomachs behind a hedge of cornstalks, we saw Old Man Kuphal step onto his porch shouldering the pellet rifle he used to pick off bluejays from his bird feeder. A squirrel guard made from a steel feed funnel clanked in the cold autumn wind. At the base of the pole lay three dead jays, their prone wings casting tiny shadows across the grass. "Run!" OB said, and, with Old Man Kuphal fixing us in his sight, we ducked beneath the Murphys' clothesline and leapt the Schweitzers' Tuscany rosebushes, which were surrounded by a moat.

Up the hill from the Fitzsimmons', the Westphals were running their sprinkler system, and every seven seconds the rotating nozzle on the southwest corner of their lot sprayed the Fitzsimmons' backyard and porch. Across the street, light from my parents' bedrooms lay on the lawn like twin tombs. Guttenoff pointed at the Lincoln Continentals parked on the Fitzsimmons' drive—one silver, the other gold—and whispered, "Her parents are home."

"Her parents are always home," OB whispered back. "They don't care if she fucks."

"How the hell do you know?" I said. "We've never seen anything."

"You haven't lived here long enough, Reville!" OB hissed. "Her parents are wacko. Bonkers. Sick as loons."

Tammy Fitzsimmon's bedroom was in the basement, and for the first time since we had begun paying our late-night visits, warm light mushroomed from her window well, drawing us over the lawn. Sunflower seeds crackled under our shoes. The wind carried sprinkler spray across our clothes. "She's down there," Guttenoff said.

We lay with our chins to the corrugated lip. Tammy sat at the foot of her bed, twisting the ends of a cigarette. Rolling-papers and a bag of pot sat beside her on peeled-back sheets. "If she lights it," Guttenoff said, "she might decide to blow the smoke out the window."

"She won't," OB said. "Her parents smoke twice as much dope as she does. They like the smell."

Tammy lit the joint with a match, and when at last she exhaled, she looked through the smoke at the reflections on the glass we lurked behind, edged backward over the bed, and lay her head on pillows. She wore a sleeveless cotton T-shirt, and while she took a second drag my eyes traveled the length of her free arm, from the black bra strap lying across the hub of her white shoulder, down the sinuous, twitching cords of muscle to her wrist and hand and the splayed folds of denim partially concealing it. Eyes closed, she unzipped her jeans, and beneath the sheen of her black panties her fingers crawled in place like a spider trapped under paint.

"What's she doing?" Pedro asked, and when nobody answered he asked again, "What's she doing?" Which was when Tammy Fitzsimmon turned off the lamp beside her bed. From the lawn we rose, cold and wet and covered with seeds.

IN THE WEEKS THAT FOLLOWED I TRIED TO FORGET OUR exploits because they so depressed me. When OB, Pedro, and Guttenoff came over, I told them I was writing a novel. Each time they came over I told them I was writing a new chapter, and eventually they stopped coming over at all. Having no friends I devoted my afternoons and evenings to school-work and earned A's on everything, which sealed me off from everybody except my teachers, who told me I was brilliant. But sometimes when I came home late after performing extra-credit dissections in Mr. Sorenson's lab, I would see OB, Pedro, and Guttenoff at the end of the block throwing a tennis ball at the sky and feel a twinge of nostalgia for the evenings we spent in front of the television, dining like emperors before the fall of Rome, engaged—vicariously but engaged no less—in sex with the biggest stars of porn.

In Islet, winds had swept off Lake Superior in the winter, fall, and spring and strafed our windows with pellets of ice. My father had designed our home with thick expansive panes, so the only rooms that did not seem like parchenko parlors were in the basement, where my mother took her address book and box of antique postcards when the first hailstones cracked against the glass. She'd grown up in southern California, and her side of the family was spread from Bakersfield to Lake Elsinor south to San Diego. When the weather turned sour, as it did even in Minneapolis where we moved as a concession to her demands for warmth, she filled in postcards to her five sisters and six brothers and, if a storm held out, to each of her nieces and nephews too.

At school I learned that our neighborhood had been a Sioux burial ground generations before Scotch-Irish farmers set plowshares into it, and so I decided to write my term paper on the Sioux uprising of 1862, which cost the lives of hundreds of white settlers and led to the largest mass execution in American history. In December of that year, a regiment of the U.S. cavalry stationed at Fort Snelling escorted thirty-eight tribesmen to Mankato, stripped them naked the day after Christmas, and with President Lincoln's sanction hung them en masse from a plywood gallows on a yellow bluff overlooking the Minnesota River.

One evening as ice hammered the yards, Tammy Fitz-simmon's father came over to our house carrying a pistol. He was a pale, portly man with thin, slicked-back hair and slack jowls that sagged over the edges of his collars like lumps in cheesecloth. "Gerald Fitzsimmon," he said. "From across the street. Connie and I wanted to welcome you to the neighborhood, but you know how time slips from one."

"Dick Reville," said my father. "My wife Jo and son Rich." My father extended his hand, and Mr. Fitzsimmon jabbed the gun barrel into my father's gut.

Though Mr. Fitzsimmon looked nothing like his daughter, the image of Tammy I saw in him—her wrists, blue-veined and tendinous where his thick, hirsute ones were; her complexion, smooth and white as bone; even her frame, so slender I wondered how a soul could reside there—so entranced me I did not even see the gun until Mr. Fitzsimmon said, "Jesus, I believe my mind's going," and set it, silver and shining, on our kitchen counter where fifty-odd postcards waited for a break in the storm. Even then, while he set three cartons of shells beside the gun, my soul's match lurked before me like a sculpture waiting to emerge from unshaped clay.

"The reason I came over," Mr. Fitzsimmon explained, "is I wondered if maybe you could keep this for me for a little while. Just until my wife feels better. See, Connie loses her temper sometimes, and I worry about her finding it. I was keeping it locked in a safe under our billiard table, but now I have reason to believe she knows the combination. It's a Llama model eight, forty-five caliber semiautomatic police weapon. Of course we all know the safest gun ever made, in the hands of the wrong person, is a very deadly weapon indeed." He gazed earnestly into my father's eyes.

My mother tended to supper, three beef Wellingtons she had placed under the broiler to brown. When she opened the oven door, smoke billowed from the delicate crusts. "Why don't you put the gun in a safe deposit box, Gerald?" my father suggested.

My mother set the baking tray and the fillets in the sink, turned on the tap, and extinguished the fires.

"I would," Mr. Fitzsimmon said, "but I can't stand bank hours." He glared at his hands and cocked his head as if he hoped words might drop from the side of his brain onto his tongue. "The truth is my wife's unstable. My daughter, well, she only salts the wounds. And I find firing the gun once or twice a month sure beats hell out of watching gold prices."

My father considered this and said, "Okay, Gerald, we'll keep it for you."

My mother turned off the faucet. "No we won't." And that was the end of the matter.

Mr. Fitzsimmon returned the bullets to his coat pocket.

Picking up the gun, he pointed the barrel at my mother's cards. "Would you like me to put those in the box?"

"Why thank you, Gerald," she said.

THAT NIGHT WHILE I WROTE MY TERM PAPER IN THE DINING room, I saw Mr. Fitzsimmon step outside onto his second-floor balcony and sip his drink in the storm. Steely wings of light radiated from the windows, transforming the house into one of those old-fashioned flying machines that never got off the ground. I had been entertaining the possibility that our neighborhood might be haunted by the indians buried beneath it and wondering if it had been good for my family ever to have left Islet, where there was nothing to do but fish, hunt, and play hockey—when curtains fluttered, and a hand, then an arm moving in silhouette above Mr. Fitzsimmon's left shoulder, closed the sliding glass door behind him. The panel in place, another hand emerged in the glass to his right and flicked down the bolt.

Mr. Fitzsimmon tried to re-enter the house. The door didn't budge, so he rapped on it, then tried to yank it across the runner. When that didn't work, he finished his drink, tossed the tumbler onto the lawn, and, while I watched it flicker across the grass and splinter on the street, he lifted one leg, then the other, over the wrought-iron railing. When he dropped, it was hard to tell whether he had fallen or the house itself had lifted, but when I looked again, he was grasping the bottom rail, his jacket vents flapping in the wind. Clearly he believed the rocks in his rock garden were feet and feet below him. They weren't. A few inches separated his wingtips from the largest of his prize collection of granite boulders, a distance he had only to stretch for. But instead he let go. His heel lodging between two rocks, his knee snapped like a bead of epoxy, and he hit the ground face first, arms and legs sprawled among the hailstones.

He got up, limped past the front of the house, not even trying the door. Just when he had eased himself behind the wheel of his gold Lincoln, Connie stepped out into the twin beams of its headlights. She wore a black negligee. As she unearthed one of the smaller boulders and carried it in her arms toward the car, her pink flanks jiggled and glowed. Mr. Fitzsimmon backed up the vehicle as Connie dipped and lobbed the rock in a granny-shot that bounced off the hood and crashed through the windshield. The car inched to a stop, the electric window lowered, and in time the boulder emerged from the chrome opening and thudded on the grass.

Gerald flung the car into reverse. Bleeding from the face, he sped unprotected into the slanting darts of ice. Mrs. Fitzsimmon walked back to the house rubbing mud from her hands. As each window went black across the street, I imagined Tammy lying on her bed in the basement, her hair splayed across three pillows, her forehead furrowed, and tried to will myself into whatever fantasy she was entertaining.

LIKE MRS. FITZSIMMON I WAS FEELING UNSTABLE MYSELF. Nights I dreamt of corpses performing fellatio, cunnilingus, and worse on one another—thousands of them in wide pits in the earth, their wrists and ankles bound with ropes, their necks collared and chained to iron capstans—and woke believing if only I told my ex-friends OB, Pedro, and Guttenoff that I was sorry for dissociating myself from them, they would say, "Don't sweat it. We've got something new we want you to see." When they had fed me the porn I craved, the dreams would fly off like bats.

But alone in the darkness, surrounded by posters of Guy LeFleur, Tony Esposito, and Bobby Orr, I sensed this would be a nostrum for a disease that had spread from the flesh to the brain to the soul, turning contentment to hunger. If I once more befriended them, what would I do in a year when OB left for college? Make sure to pocket one of his house keys, or wind up outside decrepit all-night movie palaces and bookstores with private viewing booths, trying to convince crotchety ticket vendors I was old enough to be admitted?

Luckily, the dreams and contemplations vanished on their own when varsity hockey practice began, and I could skate until the dark proclivities rose from my loins to my lungs and left through my mouthgear in trails of blood and spit. The rink was a mile from my house, across the road from the eleventh green and twelfth fairway of the country club, now as brown and windswept as the prairies south of the interstate. I rode the bus with the other players after school and in the evenings walked home between sand traps and frozen ponds, my bag of pads and leggings looped to the curve of my stick blade. I made friends who smoked dope religiously after practice, outside the pavilion between a mobile generator and a mound of ice shavings left by the Zamboni, which was parked in a prefab shed under lock and key.

Usually we had no more than a few minutes to get high, which we did with pipes made in shop class out of lug nuts and brass tubing. When the bus driver ground the gears to go, my teammates would amble to the entrance like outlaws in a podunk town, and as the taillights dipped behind trees, I would trudge through the tall, dead grass of the roughs. Grazing deer moved out of my path as I passed through their herd, and in the strip of woods behind my house I found the spinal column of a raccoon, which I took apart by the light of the moon and soaked in bleach until each vertebra was chalky and white. I strung them on a piece of rawhide and before each game hung them around my neck under my T-shirt and jersey. With each player I checked and every shot I fired, the jagged transverse, articular, and spinous processes dug into my chest like the talons of a raptor.

MY SIXTEENTH BIRTHDAY ARRIVED AT THE END OF A WEEK-long blizzard that closed schools and government agencies. On that Saturday when I entered the kitchen for breakfast, I found my father reading the morning paper, his hospital beeper lying on the kitchen table between his ashtray and coffee. "Clear the driveway," he said, "and your mother will take you to your driver's test."

I knew it was cold outside because my mother allowed my father to smoke indoors only when the mercury dipped below zero. Up and down the block neighbors cleared their drives with snowblowers, the crystal plumes rising in the shrill cold the way I imagined whale spouts might. I was rotating our blower for a final sweep when Mrs. Fitzsimmon emerged onto her stoop and called to me over the backs of two geese, a mated pair whose necks arced into drifts, hunting for buried seed. They were the only two who had not flown south with the gaggle, and my mother was certain they would both freeze to death by Christmas.

Connie squinted into the glare. She was wearing a pink and green kimono. "If you'll clear our driveway," she hollered down, "my husband will pay you a hundred dollars! Just come to the door when you're through, and he'll give you a crisp new hundred dollar note!"

"Okay!" I hollered back.

Blowing the snow from around their cars, I noticed Mr. Fitzsimmon's new windshield and hood and plush, splinter-free interior. When I rang the bell, he came to the door looking somewhat worse than his automobile, with crutches under his arms and a cast on his leg. "Yes?" he inquired, and I explained the arrangement with his wife, noting the galaxy of half-moons, cirques, and crescents drawn on his face by the spray of glass. "Come now," he said haughtily. "Surely my dear wife didn't promise you a hundred dollars."

"Pay him," came Connie's voice from inside the house. "When you have, tell him I have something to discuss with him."

I glanced at his toes, blue as robins' eggs in a nest of plaster and gauze, while he forked over five twenties from his wallet. "Evidently my wife has something to discuss with you," he said, beckoning me into the house with a sweep of his arm.

In the living room, which looked onto my house through three glass panels, Connie reclined on a Barcalounger with her coffee and paper, while Tammy, whom I had not seen except in dreams since the night I'd watched her through her window, rested on a Naugahyde couch against the wall, her hair knotted on the armrest. She smoked a cigarette, and when she saw me the smoke left her mouth in three rings that hovered for a time above the fireplace mantle, below which a pair of Duralogs smoldered. Connie removed her bifocles and set them on her wide bosom.

"I believe you and my daughter are acquainted with each other," she said. "From physiology class, taught by a Mr. Sorenson."

We were not, but I nodded anyway, to protect Tammy Fitzsimmon and thereby win her heart.

"Tammy tells me she may not be doing very well, that she may not pass. I find this hard to believe if, as she says, her attendance has been good, but no matter. She gave me this, a list of extra-credit assignments dated September third, which would be, I believe, the first day of school."

"Mother," said Tammy as Connie snapped up her glasses and put them on.

"Idea four," she read. "Visit the place of employment of someone in a health profession and write a report. It's absolutely crucial that you be polite when asking. In years past I've had students actually observe surgery."

Connie set the handout down. "Rich?" She turned to me. "Isn't your father in some sort of health profession?"

"He's an OB-GYN," I said.

"Splendid," she said. "Do you think he would mind if Tammy were to see him perform . . . oh, I don't know, some minor surgical procedure?"

"My mother spikes her coffee," Tammy interrupted. "She doesn't know what she's asking."

"I do not spike my coffee. I'm sure Dr. Reville operates on plenty of old ladies—ladies he wouldn't care if his son saw naked on an operating table."

"See," Tammy said. "I told you."

Mr. Fitzsimmon looked up from the tabloid he was reading. "You ought to listen to your mother, Tammy. She just may get you out of the mess you're in."

"So will you ask him, Richard?" Connie asked. "Politely? So he'll say yes?"

Across the street, my mother came onto the porch in a hooded snowmobile suit, matching boots and mitts, and a black Thinsulate facemask with a six-inch-long triangular snout designed by scientists to protect the faces of mountain climbers from frostbite.

"I'll ask him," I consented, aware of my mother's eyes searching for me through the eyeslits.

FOR MY BIRTHDAY SUPPER MY MOTHER HAD AGREED TO prepare some walleyes my father and I had brought back from Canada and stowed in our freezer in August. Every summer he and I drove to Thunder Bay, Ontario, hired a bushpilot to fly us, a 25-gallon barrel of gasoline, and enough staples to last a week to a fishermen's camp on Lake Pakashkan, eighty miles from any town. Inevitably, as we cast plugs from an oarboat rigged with a six-horse motor or played spades at night beneath the canvas roof of our rented shack, my father would ask me if I had any questions about sex.

No, I would tell him, and he would say, "If you ever do, Rich, you can trust me to give you the straight scoop. My profession is sex. I am a sex expert."

"I'LL FRY THEM UP," MY MOTHER SAID, EYEING THE FISH ON the kitchen counter, "but I'm not taking the skins off." So I removed the butcher paper from the thawed fillets and with a paring knife cut the skins from the meat.

My father returned from hospital rounds carrying a prophylactic box filled with store-wrapped presents, and together we helped my mother tape the last crepe paper streamer to a corner of the ceiling, then string a dozen helium balloons to my chair in the dining room. We ate, as we did most nights, in silence, only now with birthday decorations festooned above our heads. When we were through, my mother brought out the cake. It was a lemon poppy-seed sponge, with the plastic figures of a left wing and goalie stuck into the sour-cream frosting. The goalie lay face down, the left wing's stick was raised in a slapshot follow-through, and inside the net sat a chocolate puck. My father ripped down the sides of the bakery box, then asked me to blow out the candles, which I did reluctantly because I knew it would mean his proclaiming that I had no girlfriends.

"Look," he said to my mother. "No girlfriends."

"Aren't you going to open your presents, Rich?" my mother asked. When I did, the largest turned out to be a Toshiba VCR and the rest, video cassettes of box office record-breakers. *One Flew Over the Cuckoo's Nest. Jaws. E.T. The Sting.*

My father picked up the 1981 remake of *Scarface*, a movie that changed cinematic violence forever, and said, "Your mother and I wanted to start our video library with your favorite."

"I remembered your saying OB's movies were all on Beta," said my mother, "but the salesman told your father that VHS was the wave of the future. Isn't that so, sweetheart?"

"That's right," my father replied. "He told us Beta's out."

"Who cares if OB and I can't swap tapes," I said. "I sure don't."

"We love you, Rich," my mother said.

"Yes we do," my father agreed.

Then, as if I were a surfer and this conversation the only wave on a flat sea, I told my parents about Mr. Sorenson's extra-credit assignment and Mrs. Fitzsimmon's request, and I asked my father if he would allow Tammy and me into the operating room to watch him perform surgery.

For a time it was so quiet we heard the roof creaking under the weight of the snow. At last my father said he wanted to know some-thing about Tammy. "Is she a good student?" he asked.

"She's an excellent student," I lied. "She wants to *be* an OB-GYN."

"Okay, Rich." My father's voice was lowered and calm. "I want you both to meet me at the hospital annex at 6:45 Monday morn-ing. I'll be in surgery until noon. If you're late, there's nothing I can do."

"Over my dead body," my mother intoned. "Rich just turned sixteen. I'm not letting him into an operating room."

"Jo, I want my son to see what I do," my father said. "Rich, go on and phone your friend."

"Do I have any say in this?" my mother asked. "Any say at all?"

"No," he said.

"None," she stated.

"That's right." And the matter was decided.

I WENT TO THE FURNACE ROOM, AND AS I TURNED THE DIAL on an old black telephone that hung on drywall between the washer and dryer, my stomach tightened and pulse quickened as if I were performing a rite passed onto me by preceding generations, as if they watched me, deciding on the basis of one telephone call whether I was fit to propagate the race. When Mrs. Fitzsimmon answered the phone, I said, "May I speak with Tammy, please?"

"Who's calling?" she asked.

"Rich," I said. "Rich Reville from across the street." When she asked again, I said, "Dr. Reville's son."

She paused. "No, I'm afraid you may not."

"I spoke with my father," I explained. "He wants Tammy and me at the hospital annex at 6:45 Monday morning. He said we can watch him perform surgery." Hearing nothing on the line but the drums of a distant jazz orchestra, I said, "I wanted to tell Tammy I could pick her up," an offer I could make because earlier that day I had passed my driver's test with an 86.

"No need to pick her up," Mrs. Fitzsimmon replied. "Tammy's an adult. It was time she moved into her own apartment."

"You mean to tell me Tammy doesn't live with you anymore?" I asked, astonished.

"Tammy moved out weeks ago. She lives uptown now. I thought you knew that. At 35th and Portland."

"35th and Portland? The hospital is at 35th and Portland."

"That's why you won't need to pick her up. She lives across the street from the hospital."

"Will you tell her I'll meet her there?"

"She's to meet you," Mrs. Fitzsimmon said, "at 6:45 Monday morning at the hospital annex."

"That's right," I said and hung up the phone believing I had charmed the dead.

AT THE HOSPITAL MY FATHER REPORTED THAT TAMMY AND I were med students from the University of Minnesota, fell in love with his own lie, and seemed to convince himself that this was true. He sat across from the patient in a small consultation chamber three levels below the ground, and Tammy and I stood in the doorway in white coats he had gotten from a lab. "They'll be in the operating room with me," my father told the woman, "along with the anesthesiologist and the surgical assistants you met in the hallway."

The patient nodded. Like many of the patients my father treated at the free clinic where he and his medical partners practiced one night a month, she was a Native American, no older than twenty, and pretty, with teeth straighter and whiter than mine and braided hair the color of black earth.

"They're top of their class," my father continued—so handsome in his gray suit and red tie I wished my mother could see him.

While he finished talking with the patient, Tammy and I waited for him in a lounge across the hall. She lit a cigarette. "It's bizarre to think," she said, "that I had life sucked out of me down here, perhaps on the other side of that wall."

"You mean you had an abortion?" I asked in amazement.

"Last summer," she answered. "I remember the day perfectly. There was a moving van parked in your driveway. You were sitting on the lip when my boyfriend Lou picked me up in his Rambler. I dumped that son of a bitch."

"So you didn't need to come here to write a report. You have the firsthand experience."

"Fucking right," she said. "But I'm not writing a report about it."

"But you could've."

"You mean Sorenson?" she asked. "Sorenson wouldn't pass me if I observed a brain transplant. If you think that, you're as deluded as my poor mother." She flung back her hair, and a silver chain glimmered against her clavicle, and even that seemed wondrous. "Unh-unh," she announced. "I'm here to fuck your father."

I paused. "What did he do to you?"

"He didn't do anything to me," she said. "I'm infatuated with him. Have been since the day Sorenson told how he delivered their little girl. Sure, I'd noticed your father before that. Who wouldn't?

In the first part of the summer when he was living in the house alone, and I'd see him in the evening watering the shrubs, or shooting baskets by himself on the driveway, or washing his car by hand, he did those things so tenderly it didn't surprise me he delivered babies for a living. Even before I knew what he did, I imagined what it would be like to bed him."

"He's married," I said.

"Your mother doesn't love him. And he doesn't love your mother. That was apparent the day you moved in." She paused, and I took in the sheen of her patent leather pumps and the tiny green and yellow marionettes printed into the silk of her blue skirt, and I thought how none of it was meant for me. "At first I thought about seeing him at his office," she went on, "but I figured he probably had a policy against becoming romantically involved with patients."

"I can't believe you went to such planning," I said. In truth, I couldn't comprehend it, the months that had gone into it.

"I didn't plan anything. Everything just fell into place more or less." She put her cigarette out in an ashtray, tapped another from the pack as my father came into the lounge holding a cigarette, too. He lit hers, then lit his own.

"So the patient has a benign teratoma on her left ovary," she said, "a cyst that develops out of genetic material."

My father nodded, pleased his description of what we would see had not fallen on deaf ears.

"By what method did you discover it, Dr. Reville?" she asked, and as he told her about the patient's bloatedness and nausea and the laparoscopy he had performed the week before, I succumbed to the vision before me, saw her not as she was but as she wanted my father to see her. In the clothes she'd chosen, in the makeup she'd put on, in the interest she wore on her face like a mask, she might have passed for his assistant or even his partner. The smoke from their cigarettes encompassing us, I felt as if I were no longer there, as if the flesh had been seared from the soul and I lurked in the room as a presence, a chill, a shadow cast by no physical object.

"A laparoscopy," my father explained, "is an exploratory procedure. Imagine a telescope the size of a number two pencil. That's a laparoscope. It's inserted into the patient's abdomen through a tiny incision. The doctor can look through it directly or see what's inside the body on a television monitor."

"Fascinating," Tammy said, and I saw how my father's pleasure showed through his composure.

When they were done with their cigarettes, my father ushered us down a narrow corridor to the men's and women's scrubrooms. "I asked Dr. Sing here at OR to help you with a locker and scrub suit, Tammy," he said. "She's waiting for you inside."

"Thanks," she replied.

Inside the scrubroom, as my father and I undid our ties and hung our suits in lockers, I wanted to tell him that I'd lied about Tammy, that she was not an excellent student and had no intention of becoming an OB-GYN, and that she had designs on him beyond his wildest imaginings, but I had never talked to my father about anything of importance, not even when we were fishing, and each sentence I formed in my head sounded more ridiculous than the one before it.

"I'm going to tell you something I probably shouldn't, Rich," my father said as we washed our hands in a basin. "After you and Tammy left the consultation, the patient asked about you. I think she was taken with you. She wanted to know your name."

"Did you tell her?" I asked.

"Of course not. But I wanted you to see that patients are people. After years of practicing medicine, some doctors forget this."

By the time we entered the operating room the patient had been anesthetized and lay beneath operating lamps. A brownish stain between her navel and the edge of her pubic bush marked the spot to be opened. My father stepped between her legs, which were spread apart by table-extenders. On either side of him female assistants waited with hemostats, needle-holders, cochers, and scalpels. I stood beside Tammy, who stood beside one of them. We were high-school students, but we were dressed like everyone in the room except for the patient—in lime scrubs, latex gloves, and surgical masks.

As my father made the incision, I watched his fingers, fingers I'd felt lovingly against my scalp since before I could remember, but fingers I could not remember ever touching my mother, not to brush the hair from her face or zip up the back of her dress. The incision made, my father applied metal clamps to the flaps of skin, then stanched the flow of blood with small electric shocks administered through a hand-held cauterizer. It was connected by a cord to a pedal on the floor, and each time he pressed it, the cauterizer made the same buzzing sound as a backyard mosquito zapper. The ovarian cyst was immediately identifiable. It was yellow and glistening and larger than everything else around it. A grapefruit-sized egg yolk covered with veins, black follicles of hair, and small, tooth-like deposits of bone. In the open air of the operating room, it sagged lopsidedly, but in the tight enclosure of the human body it slid among organs and glands and occupied the slick crannies between viscera.

My father pushed it aside, applied his scalpel to the stretch of tissue at its base, and severed it from the ovary.

"You've just witnessed the removal of a benign teratoma," he said and dropped it in a stainless steel bowl held out to him by the assistant nearest me. She in turn set the bowl on a steel cart behind her.

"Bravo, Dr. Reville," said the anesthesiologist, a burley, dark-eyed man with a beard that curled out like weeds from the edges of his surgical mask.

My father pulled back the edges of the opening and pointed out the patient's pancreas, bladder, and colon. "Everything looks pretty much just as it's drawn in the textbooks, doesn't it?" he said, then plied a needle through the flaps of skin and narrowed the incision with a knot.

I did not answer yes or no to this. Nor did Tammy, who hovered over the cyst as if transfixed by it, as if in its sheen she saw her own perfectly beautiful face transmogrified.

"Is she all right?" the anesthesiologist asked. He stood beside the patient's head, his eyes wide, concerned, as Tammy cupped the cyst in her palms.

My father craned his neck over his assistant's shoulder. "It's okay, Arny," he said. "She can examine it if she wants."

I touched Tammy's arm. She was not okay. Her body was rigid, her breaths frenetic. Her hair was tied and netted, and from the sliver of flesh behind her ear came the smell of jonquils, delicate and almost undetectable, and I wanted to kiss that spot, to graze it ever so lightly with my lips. "Set the teratoma back in the dish," I whispered. "You don't want to look at it." Fluid seeped between her fingers into the bowl. With her thumbs she parted its hair and caressed its teeth. "Please," I said. "For your own good."

I placed my hands on its warm surface, sank my fingers into its sides, and Tammy tightened her grip, the skin of the thing bulging against my palms. In a second we had cored it. She held one half, I the other. In the half she held, nestled in a network of veins, a nugget of blood lay, a capsule hard and dark as a ruby.

"There's a strange beauty in the rampant," said my father. He had finished his sewing and stood behind us—a professor who'd inadvertently stumbled onto his students with a botched experiment. Perhaps it was what he said. Perhaps it was simply the calmness of his voice, but Tammy's eyes released their hold, and when her half of the teratoma had slid from her fingers into the bowl, I set mine on top of it.

When my father asked if we'd had enough surgery for one morning, I told him I had, and Tammy told him that she had not.

"I've got a tubal ligation followed by a vaginal hysterectomy followed by a second tubal," he told her.

"After that what?" she asked.

"Nothing," my father said. "I've got nothing after that."

"Good," she said, and I left them there in the operating room. I know no more than this: that when I got home I asked my mother to call the high school and tell the secretary I was ill, that in the evening my father called to tell my mother to go to bed without him, which she did most nights anyway. I told her nothing about what had happened at the hospital, and she didn't ask, and together we watched *Scarface*, which wasn't nearly as frightening as I remembered it.

LONG AFTER MY PARENTS' DIVORCE WAS PEACEABLY HANDLED by their respective attorneys and they had both remarried, Gerald shot Connie five times in the arms, legs, and chest with a forty-five caliber handgun. I was living in San Francisco at the time, lying in bed with the woman who would eventually become my ex-wife Joy, when my father phoned to tell me the news. He had been driving home at two or three in the morning after a night of deliveries when he came to a police roadblock at our end of Braemar Court. By then the ambulance had taken Connie away from the scene of the shooting, and as an officer signaled my father into our driveway, he saw Gerald leave in the backseat of a squad car. Two weeks later, when Connie recovered enough to remember what had happened, she dropped all charges against her husband, who claimed he'd fired on her in self-defense.

Mr. and Mrs. Fitzsimmon still live across the street from my dad. I don't know what became of OB, Pedro, and Guttenoff, but a few weeks after the operation I discovered plates of Christmas cookies my mother had baked for them—krumkaken and pfeffernusse, nut tarts and lemon squares—each wrapped in plastic and topped with a bow.

"No way," I said when I saw their names, each written on a card in my mother's fine cursive. "I'm not taking these to them."

"No one's asking you to," she said, but when I imagined what she might see through their doorways, I went for my jacket and boots.

Outside, the sky was gray and snow was falling. I handed Guttenoff's plate to his father, who came onto the stoop in Nikes and a bathrobe. I set Pedro's inside his storm door, for I knew the wrestling team was in Iowa and I didn't want to disturb his mother, whom I could hear mumbling inside the house. Climbing the drive to the geodesic dome, I considered feeding OB's cookies to the deer. He was the sickest of the three, but also the most sensitive, and I dreaded seeing him most of all.

When he came to the door, we faced each other without speaking for what seemed like hours, then I handed him the gift my mother had baked for him.

"Want to watch one of my father's documentaries?" he asked. When I didn't answer, he said matter-of-factly, "He doesn't make pornos."

"Okay," I said.

Spread out on the carpet were video cassettes labeled "Bats in Ecuador," "Sloths in Costa Rica," "Tapirs in Sabah and Sarawak."

"He makes them for zoos all over the world," OB explained, returning from the kitchen with paté fresh from the deli. "Animals mate differently in the wild than in captivity, so the zoos fly him in to each animal's natural habitat, to capture how they really do it, when no one's watching."

On the screen a female ape scurried away from her sex partner, so he grabbed another by the shoulders and thrust himself in her. Outside, the wind whipped snow from the trees, and I wondered whom I would one day meet and what she'd be like.

THE NIGHT MY BROTHER WORKED THE HEADER

Last day of the salmon season, Old Windell gave a knife to Larry Olseth and put him on the butcher line next to me. "Be nice to him, Agnes," Windell said. The salmon dropped every three and a half seconds from the stainless steel header and crowded through the open gate as if still alive. They plopped onto the belt headless, one to a slot. We kept up pretty well. Uma-san and Saka-san, the Japanese butchers, slit the bellies, throats, and bloodlines. I separated the egg sacs from the guts and dropped them down the metal chute to the egg house. The sacs toppled into the flow like lopped-off pairs of orange fingers and disappeared around the first bend in the rickety converted rain gutter. Windell winked at me.

"OK, Agnes?" he said.

"OK," I answered.

"Aa-o!" sang Paolo, the big Filipino slimer at the end of the belt.

"Aa-o!" sang Dung-Dong, the old Vietnamese scraper two positions down. On the butcher line, that's how we talked, a sung language. But as soon as Larry Olseth started butchering fish, the singing stopped. He stood on the line between Uma-san and me, as tall and awkward as an ostrich. His thin wrists stuck out from his sleeves like bare bones. His blond, feathery-haired head stuck a foot above everybody else's, on a neck as thin and gristly as boat line. He was cute enough, but he'd never butchered salmon before. Uma-san let him try every sixth fish, and believe me, it wasn't pretty. He gouged stomachs open and ripped into meat. He wrecked egg sacs without blinking an eye. When he told me he loved me, I nearly grabbed his knife and slit his throat.

We were processing grade-A sockeye salmon, the only fish that came to our cannery and freezer plant that were anywhere near good enough to vacuum-pack in cellophane and sell to the Japanese. Most of the fish we got were soft, smelly chum salmon, silver salmon bloated with gas, humpy salmon falling off the bone and covered with growths. Sometimes we got king salmon that were as large as men; they smelled worse by far than any other fish, on account of the extra meat. But the salmon on the belt that morning were fine, marvelous fish that shimmered under the overhead lights. Were it not for the blood that drained from their necks and bellies, they might've passed for fish brooches inlaid with turquoise and quartz, like those worn by women east of here, in places like Wrangell and Ketchikan.

So we handled them with care. No one wanted to bruise a freezer fish. Old Windell had told us at breakfast he would be counting the number of fish Ido-san, the Japanese grader, tossed into the plastic tote marked CANNERY. We had to be careful, he said, if we wanted our jobs back next season. Every fish that went to the cannery troughs, through the washers, fin shredders and rotary mincers, every fish that got stuffed into a can, sent down the chinks over the weights and scales, down the long, greased rail into the 500-gallon pressurized steam cooker, meant a loss for the company. "Add it up," he told us. "Weigh it against the cost of labor. Anybody here think he's inexpendable?"

"I said I love you, Agnes." Larry Olseth had blue eyes that could turn a person to stone.

"I heard you," I said.

There was a huge glassless window on the butcher line. During the winter you could look though it to the sea, but in salmon season it was blocked by two stainless steel crab cookers, one stacked on top of the other. The morning Larry Olseth started butchering, a sunbeam passed over the top of them and made a rectangle of light on the belt between him and me. The salmon moved into it and became flames I wanted to touch, not through gloves with cotton liners, but with bare hands. But I'd handled enough fish to know how cold and wet they were. Fingering the rough skin would have only wrecked the illusion. To me the salmon looked foil-wrapped, as beautiful as the chocolate Christmas fish the outpost store in Ahkiok received each year in time for Lent.

"Leave with me tomorrow on the plane," Larry Olseth said. I knew, without having to look up, that he was making himself look more pitiful than any dog in our village.

I was glad Carl was out of earshot. I didn't want my brother, the butcherline foreman, thinking anything funny was going on. Five feet above the rest of us, on a platform made out of pine boards and reinforced metal, he operated the salmon header, a circular saw for taking the heads off fish. From where I stood on the line, I could see him out of the corner of my eye, in yellow rain pants and brown plaid shirt, his braid coiled snakelike in a hairnet that hung outside his collar, his thumbs hooked in the gills of a sockeye salmon. His job was to clamp the fish into the six spring-loaded adjustable collars on the crown of the header and make sure none of them fell off before hitting the sixteen-inch circular blade. Loaded with salmon, the header looked like one of those merry-go-rounds at the fair, the kind with swings, only when the fish got three quarters of the way around, they dropped like sausage links onto a tray table and their heads tumbled down a wooden slide into a 4 x 4 plastic tote.

"We'll live with my friends Eric and Fran," Larry Olseth said. "They're spray-paint artists. They've got a studio next to the electrical plant in Union Way. Wait till you see it, Agnes. Graffiti poems on the walls and ceiling. Paintings of shrunken heads and bicycle handlebars. Eric's got one of a fire hydrant, and all around it are these yellow cats. Not dogs but cats. It's terrific. He's got it displayed in their bedroom, under the basketball hoop."

"Someone's missing throats!" Dung-Dong accused, and he didn't mean Uma-san and Saka-san.

"Throat, throat, throat," his brother Hwen-Mao repeated. "Three throats!"

Larry Olseth stopped humming a song when he told me we'd hike the Tibetan plain. "I've got a friend by the name of Arun. He owns a restaurant in Mussoorie, India. We'll leave from his place. Think of it, masala dosa for lunch, tandoori chicken for dinner. In the evenings we'll bathe in the headwaters of the Ganges, pray to the sacred Siva, sleep under the Hindu heaven. Imagine, Agnes, riding a one-humped camel, meals served to us on banana leaves, sipping arrack and reading Upanishads to each other until dawn."

The crew was quickly becoming annoyed. No one liked the looks of Larry Olseth's fish. We kept looking down the belt to see how Ido-san was grading them. If too many fish went into the wrong tote, we might have to find new jobs. Windell wouldn't fire a college boy, we knew that, even if he sent 5000 fish to the cannery. Larry Olseth butchered in jerks, as if he were gutting a deer. He shoved in the knife the way you would bust open a sternum, and carved mouths in the gullets, complete with curling lips. After a while, I had to stop watching him.

"Cut the throats!" Dung-Dong ordered.

"The bloodlines!" Hwen-Mao added. "Cut the bloodlines!"

"This is what we'll do," Larry Olseth crooned. "We'll stock a cupboard with sex tools. Vibrators, dildos, fruit-flavored jellies. We'll use only condoms with nubbins on them, and we'll videotape our sexcapades. In Korea, Agnes, men and women pull strings of pearls out of each other. We can order them through the mail. I'll get two, one for each of us."

"Look," I said, holding up a fish. Eggs poured out its open neck like bath oil beads. "I'm behind because of you."

Dung-Dong was losing his patience. "Goddamn," he muttered and shook his head. "Goddamn."

Paolo's voice boomed from the end of the line. "Too much blood in the fish!"

"Goddamn." Dung-Dong couldn't scrape out the blood if the bloodlines weren't cut. The fish with guts in them were two slots from Hwen-Mao's scraping spoon. Between them and me were no fewer than six fish.

Larry Olseth turned his eyes on me. They were as blue as a pair of marbles. "What's eating you, Agnes?" he asked. Just then, I backed into the steel toe of Hwen-Mao's rubber boot and landed flat on my back on the carpet of guts. Spleens and intestines covered my face. Larry Olseth offered me his hand.

"Stop the belt!" Hwen-Mao shouted when he opened a fish and found its guts and eggs intact.

Carl turned off the belt and came around the far end of the header. "What's going on?" he asked, picking up an end wrench from the box of tools and slapping it in his palm a few times. No one wanted to annoy Carl. He was strong enough to throw a wrench five times the length of the one in his hand, sure-sighted enough to hit an empty beer can with it from twelve yards. When Carl was fifteen, Windell caught him with his daughter up on Alitak mountain, fucking on the fat slab of rock next to the fallen-down radio tower. Windell marched him down the side of the mountain back to the cannery, a rifle barrel pointed at his head. That night he handcuffed Carl to the flagpole and, in the morning, made Carl watch a helicopter lift off with the girl in the cockpit. The next summer, Windell promoted Carl to foreman. At nineteen, he was a better foreman than men twice his age.

"The new guy," Dung-Dong said.

"What new guy?" Carl asked. He knew who Dung-Dong was talking about, but playing stupid was part of the game. Most of the people on the butcher line couldn't have explained a situation in English to save their lives, which was why we made such an effort to get along.

"The new guy," Dung-Dong repeated, and motioned with his head.

Carl looked at Larry Olseth, but his back was turned, helping me pick gonads and bladders off my jacket. Anger flashed in my brother's eyes, but Larry Olseth was as oblivious to it as a fish on the belt. "I'd like to take you right here, Agnes. Right here in the guts," Larry Olseth whispered. Carl lowered himself from the plat-form, came up to me on the other side of the belt and slid two slick fingers underneath my chin.

"You all right, Agnes?" he asked.

"Yes, Carl," I said, pushing Larry Olseth away.

"You fall by accident, or somebody push you?"

"Nobody pushed me, Carl."

He sneered at me. "You need to be meaner," he said.

One of the ways he had tried to make me meaner was by putting the barrel of a deer rifle to my temple. "Look out the win-dow and make up a story," he would say, punching out the safety on the magazine. And looking into the winter fog, which rose up out of the sea as thick as grass, I would begin a story about the Japanese glass float, the plastic doll's leg, or teacup handle of Chinese porcelain—all bits of exotic jetsam I'd discovered while digging for steamer clams. But before I could get past the setting, he would make the hammer click-click-click in the hollow cham-ber. "You're boring me, Agnes," he would say. He believed that to live year round in Ahkiok, Alaska, a person had to be mean. I believed a person mustn't get bored.

He withdrew his fingers, which left my throat wet. I watched him grab the rail of the platform and pull himself up. When Carl was halfway back, Dung-Dong said, "Aren't you going to say some-thing to the new guy?"

Carl spun around. He thought a moment. "I might tell Windell Dung-Dong's getting too old to work."

"I'm not too old!" Dung-Dong shrieked. It was true some refugees worked until they were a hundred.

Carl started up the header. "Life's short, Agnes," Larry Olseth said. The fish came one to a slot, packed in as tight as the links on a watchband. Larry Olseth said, "All right, Agnes. I'll do the job right."

"You couldn't if you tried," I said.

"Oh, yeah?"

"Yeah," I said.

But he did. He bowed to Uma-san and asked him to teach him the Japanese way of salmon butchering. Uma-san raised his eyebrows so they looked like little V-shaped temples. "Japanese way?" he asked.

"Yes," Larry Olseth said.

I was amazed. Larry Olseth's fish improved as soon as Uma-san showed him how to hold the knife and glide the blade. He slit the throats, bellies, and bloodlines perfectly, so that the egg sacs slid out as smoothly as Popsicles. We were happy. Hwen-Mao and Dung-Dong scraped the snakes of blood off the spinal cords and flung them at Chung-Soo when he came to collect the tote of fish heads. "Good job, Larry," Uma-san said. Paolo's voice boomed in song.

For a while harmony united us, from the slimers and scrapers on up the line to me, the egg-puller. I asked Larry Olseth, "Why'd Windell put you on the butcher line? You've never even butchered before."

"Because I asked him to," he replied.

"And he just did it?"

"Sure. I told him I was in love with you, Agnes. I said, 'Listen, Windell, if you don't let me butcher fish next to Agnes Agnug, it'll be your fault if I leave tomorrow and never see her again.' He said, 'You're absolutely right, Larry. If I did that to you, I'd be unable to sleep nights, I'd be so disgusted with myself. I'll put you on the butcher line first thing after ten o'clock mug-up.'"

I shook my head.

"Seriously, Agnes. I asked him to put me here and he did."

That didn't surprise me. The college boys wore caps advertising the names of their fathers' firms: National Can Company, American Clip Manufacturers, Mermaid Ocean Delicacies. Larry Olson's cap said CRYOVAC, the company that made the bags we froze the fish in. Still, it angered me.

Larry Olseth said, "Leave with me tomorrow and you'll never be poor."

"But I don't love you," I said.

"You don't?"

"No," I said.

"But you told me you did."

TRUE. THREE NIGHTS EARLIER I HAD TOLD LARRY OLSETH I loved him. How it happened was, I was sitting on his bed when he handed me a mirror with two big lines of cocaine on it. "Use this," he said and handed me a rolled-up $100 bill. We took turns snorting, and when we were through he set up two more lines and told me I could have them both. I did, and when they were gone I thought I'd never seen a more handsome boy.

I said, "Let's go for a walk on the pier." He slipped a pint of Johnnie Walker into his jacket and held the door open for me. Outside the dorm a big full moon had risen over the ocean. I said, "The killer whales will be feeding tonight."

We sipped whiskey as we passed the machine shop. Through the cracked window the drill presses and band saws looked like people hunched over in the darkness, but I wasn't afraid. I'd walked to the end of the pier plenty of nights—sometimes alone. In front of the freezer, I bit Larry Olseth's ear and told him, "Put your arm around me, Larry." He did, and I asked him if he wanted to go to a place only I knew about, a secret place under the dock.

"Yes," he said, and I led him by the hand to the slippery wooden ladder at the end of the pier.

The rungs were wet and cold. When I came within three feet of the glistening water, I called up to him, "Come on, Larry." As I reached with my foot for the slick plank, I could see him start down the ladder, one foot at a time, the soles of his sneakers flitting between the rungs like ghosts. I gripped the rope railing and balanced across the narrow beam, crunching barnacles under my boots, to the bed made out of old two-by-fours. "Come on," I urged. A good two feet above the high-water mark, the bed was the perfect place to keep blankets and cigarettes. I reached for Larry Olseth and he handed me the bottle and climbed in next to me. Above us moonlight filtered through planks in the pier, making bars across our faces. Below us, we heard a swish in water, killer whales drawn to the shimmering schools of Dolly Vardens under the dock. I said, "Kiss me, Larry." He unzipped my pants. "Yes, finger me, Larry." And while he did, I said I loved him.

AT THE END OF THE LINE, PAOLO SANG A LOVE SONG WITH French words in it. Larry Olseth butchered only every fifth fish, but they were turning out as good as either Uma-san's or Saka-san's, so Uma-san asked him to try every fourth fish. "OK," Larry Olseth agreed.

"*You're the little girl that I adore*," sang Paolo.

"Love needs time to evolve," Larry Olseth said. "It doesn't happen overnight. Like a seed it needs to be nurtured, watered, given sunlight."

"I could never love you," I said.

"Then forget about love. Think of the drugs."

I DID. UNDERNEATH THE PIER, I TOLD LARRY OLSETH ABOUT the deaths, about kids I knew killing themselves for no reason. Most of them did it in the winter, when the horizontal rains slashed against the aluminum siding of the houses for months at a time and no one had any hope of cocaine coming around until May. A boy told his family he was going out to kill a deer. A girl said she was going for a walk and her father hung the rifle on her shoulders for protection against bears. They'd place the end of the barrel against the roof of their mouth and push the trigger with their thumbs. I told Larry Olseth to imagine ripping planks for coffin wood from the floors of the abandoned seiners south of the cannery. That's what little kids in the village did. I told Larry Olseth about the suicides of E. J., Myra, and T. Pontiac, and before that of Rhoda, Ewell, and Buster, kids who had climbed up the mountain out of the world. Then I told him what I had told many people, that the way to end all the discontent and needless destruction of our youth was to maintain a steady flow of drugs into our community year round.

"*I love you, I love you, I lo-o-ve you,*" PAOLO SANG. THINGS were going fine. Only diseased fish went to the cannery. Ido-san sent the rest to the freezer.

"We send the coke third-class parcel post," Larry Olseth said. "It's cheap. Nobody checks it. It gets here."

Uma-san said, "Real good, Larry. Real good." He was referring to Larry Olseth's fish, which were good, *mostly*. A couple of times, I noticed a throat or a bloodline that wasn't cut all the way, but I wasn't going to say anything about a couple of salmon. For never having butchered before, he was doing a very good job. Uma-san raised his eyebrows. "You try every third fish, Larry?"

"Sure," Larry Olseth agreed, and Uma-san made a joke in Japanese that I didn't understand.

Larry had to work his knife fast now, and some of his cuts were a little sloppy. "Your dream, Agnes. You said it was a sign."

YES. UNDERNEATH THE PIER I HAD TOLD LARRY OLSETH about the night last March when T. Pontiac came to my house all drunk, asking me whether I had anything to smoke. Just cigarettes, I whispered. He wanted sheesh, he said. But he stood in the kitchen anyway, eyeing me as if I were the drugs themselves. I pushed him toward the door. From inside his jacket, he pulled out a pack of Viceroys. They were drenched through. He said he was going to smoke them one after another until they were gone, and then he was going up the mountain to blow off his head.

I said, Not now, Pontiac, you'll wake people. We both laughed hard—but quietly—so we wouldn't wake people. So many kids had killed themselves, mentioning it was almost a joke between us. Pontiac kissed me on the mouth and left through the side door into the rain.

I crawled into bed with my sister's baby. Carol had won a scholarship to pharmacology school in Anchorage, so every night for the months that she was away I put her little girl, Sarah, between my breasts and went to sleep to the little puffs of air, in and out. When the gun went off, I dreamed I'd been shot through the heart. I felt the penetration of the bullet and the flip of my body onto the pebbles. I looked up and seven hunters in mukluks formed a circle around me. A boy with feathery blond hair knelt beside me. Move her from the spot and she'll die, said the boy. He stood me up on the stones to show them. Thank you, I said, thank you very much. When I awoke in the morning, no one had to tell me that Pontiac was dead, for I knew it as if I had seen a vision.

"REMEMBER, AGNES," LARRY OLSETH SAID. "UNDERNEATH the pier. You told me I was the blond-haired boy of your dream. You can't deny it. You said it was a sign."

"A sign of what?" I asked.

"How should I know?" Larry Olseth missed some more throats and bloodlines. He cut them, just not deeply enough, so the egg sacs came apart in my glove. Still, I said nothing. He was trying to do a good job.

"Very fast learner, Larry." Uma-san could say that because he didn't have to pull the egg sacs or scrape the blood from fish that were only half finished. Then he said, "I leave now. Bye-bye, Larry," and set down his knife. "You butcher with Saka-san. Every other fish. Japanese." Taking off his apron, he made another joke that nobody except Saka-san understood, then removed his gloves and hung them on the wall behind him. He was done for the summer. Even though it wasn't quite noon, he was going to Japan House to pack his things for the flight to Tokyo in the morning. As he walked through the fork gate behind the header, the fish rolled upon Larry Olseth like waves, pushing him like a raft at sea, until he was butchering fish right next to me, jamming me in the ribs with his elbow.

"Throat!" Dung-Dong said.

"Bloodline!" Hwen-Mao said.

"Agnes," said Larry Olseth. None of the throats and bloodlines were cut now. Sac upon sac ripped in my glove. "Leave with me. It's written in the cosmos. It's meant to be."

Two more sacs ripped in my glove. "I'll leave with you, Larry"—these were my exact words—"when all the throats are cut!"

My brother Carl looked at me from the header. All he had heard me say was that I'd leave with Larry.

AROUND THREE IN THE AFTERNOON WE FINISHED BUTCHER-ing the last tote of salmon. Carl told us that before we could leave we had to sweep all the guts into the drains, hose down the header, belt, and tray tables, and sponge mop all the fish scales off the butcher-line wall. I beat Dung-Dong to the broom, which meant the old Vietnamese had to wipe down the header, an OK job if Paolo kept the fire hose down. Carl started up the crown lift, forked the tote of fish heads and drove off to dump it from the end of the pier. While the rest of us worked, Larry Olseth leaned against a runner of the garage door, smoked cigarettes, and stared at me with his blue eyes. He had kept up all afternoon, the same as Saka-san. Once he'd adjusted to the pace, nobody could complain about his work, not me, not Dung-Dong, not Hwen-Mao.

I kept my eyes on my broom. The purple livers, floppy white gonads and pink strings of tissue swirled like sunset clouds in the whirlpools above the drains. Larry Olseth was going to leave tomorrow on the plane. I had that thought as I swept out fish heads from underneath the belt and sent them coasting off the end of my broom like shuffleboard pucks. I aimed them at the drains, where they plopped through to the ocean below. Maybe we could be pen pals for a year or two—until we forgot the looks of each other's faces.

"Goddamn."

I looked up. Mario, the quiet slimer, was talking to Paolo about orange-picking in Stockton, California, where the Filipinos spent the nine months they didn't spend here. This sort of thing happened every day. Paolo got interested in something someone was saying and forgot he was holding the fire hose. My face had been blasted plenty of times. This time, though, it was Dung-Dong. The water came straight up and exploded off his face like fireworks.

Of the twenty or so people who had seen Dung-Dong carried off the line on a stretcher two seasons earlier with a collapsed aorta, not one stepped in to do anything. Larry Olseth, of all people, pushed the fire hose down, and when he did, Paolo said, "Keep your hands off me, you white fucker." His stomach was as big around as a backyard cooker.

The old Vietnamese climbed down off the platform, his hair as wet and bristly as a newly hatched bird. "Where's Carl?" he asked. "He'll take that goddamned thing out of your hands."

Paolo called the old man a cocksucker and held the nozzle level with the crotch of his rain pants. Dung-Dong made a beeline for the garage door, his wrinkled face trembling like fish wrap in the breeze. Larry Olseth followed him out the door and leaned against a stack of pallets. It made me sick to think he was above having to help us with cleanup.

I climbed the header platform to finish wiping off the scales and blood from the collars, crown, and blade. I loosened the bolt on the blade and took it off so that I could pick out the globs of guts that were wrapped around the rotisserie like rubber bands. Dung-Dong returned as I was tightening the blade down. "I thought you went to get Carl," Paolo said.

"Carl went to the village," Dung-Dong said. "I saw him in his skiff." Ahkiok was four miles away by water, which meant Carl had left for the day.

"No!" Paolo beamed.

"Go ahead, call me a liar." Dung-Dong sounded like he didn't care anymore.

The fire hose twisted on the floor like a snake. "Another day, another dollar," Paolo said as he turned off the water. I climbed off the platform, though I hadn't finished cleaning it, walked past the fish house, the egg house, the freezer plant, but I found only Carl's crown lift, plugged into a socket in the side of the warehouse, and the hosed-out tote drying in the sun. In the slip where Carl tied up the skiff each morning hung the bowline. Its frayed end wafted back and forth in the current like hair, entangling the legs of starfish stuck to the piling. Normally, he wound and tied the rope and set it neatly under the seat.

"Agnes." I felt Larry Olseth's cool hands soft as a down-filled hood over my ears. "I'm gone from here."

"What do you mean?" I asked, trying to size him. He had dark plates under his eyes that made him look charming and pitiful at the same time.

"I'm here," he said, "but really I'm not." He put a wad of Red Man as big as a jaw-breaker inside his lip. "Though I'm here, I'm eons from here, off the coast of Egypt where Odysseus' men ate lotus leaves and dreamed of mountains and waterfalls so real they wanted to stay there." He cleared his throat and drooled a string of saliva a foot long off the end of the pier.

"So I'm saving that old Vietnamese man's life back there—what's-his-name, Ding-Bat. But what I'm thinking about is this thing I read about how botanists identified a certain hallucinogenic fern they believed to be the actual lotus eaten by the mariners. You saw that Filipino giant. He wanted to rend me limb from limb, but what I'm thinking about, Agnes, is picking the little ferns and stuffing them in my bag."

"Come on," I said. "Let's get out of here."

"All right," he said. We took off our rain gear and boots, hung our pants and jackets on nails in the cloakroom, clipped our gloves to the clothesline. I asked Larry Olseth whether he had any more coke.

"Of course," he said. So we walked side by side in broad daylight past the open door of the machine shop, past the high-pitched whir of the power grinder, past the flying sparks of old Dan the machinist. We walked through the center of the mess hall, past Tiny, the head cook, singing, "Doo-doo-doo-didlee-doo-didlee-doo-doo!" He would be gone tomorrow. At the top of the stairs, we walked past work boots, deck boots, tennis shoes, past coveralls hanging from hooks and spotted with grease. No girls or women were allowed in the men's dorm. That was Windell's law. Larry Olseth opened the door to room six.

"We should be quiet," I said. Larry Olseth locked the door. Underwear, socks, shampoo, washcloths lay on his bed ready to be packed. I moved a couple of his shirts and made a place for myself on the bedspread. He opened the drawer of the bureau, removed a blue bag with a black drawstring. Inside it were the mirror and the canister of coke. "Tomorrow, Agnes, I'll be back in Seattle." He dumped some of the chunky white powder onto the mirror and began to chop it with a razor blade. We spoke through our noses because a misdirected breath could send the particles flying. "The first place I'm going," Larry Olseth said, "is Umberto's Italian Ice. For some raspberry." With the edge of the razor he made four thick lines. "You ever wanted something so bad you could taste it?" he asked.

"It wasn't raspberry," I said.

"Coke whore," Larry Olseth said. He handed me the mirror and the rolled-up bill. I snorted my lines a third at a time, each one a burst of coolness like a breeze in my head, like the mist that curls off the breakers at high tide. I asked whether there was more.

"More what?"

"You know," I said.

"What's left on the mirror. Go ahead, lick it off." I did, and felt the tingle on my gums and tongue as I reached for the fly of Larry Olseth's jeans.

WE AWOKE AT THREE A.M. TO CARL'S POUNDING. HE WANTED us to let him in or he'd blow down the door.

"What do you want?" Larry Olseth asked. My hand rested on his bare chest. My lips were next to his ear.

"I'm going to hide in the closet," I told him. "If Carl finds me here, he'll cut me into strips and stuff me into a crab pot."

Larry Olseth looked at me. "I'm serious," I said.

"Let me in," Carl said. As quietly as I could, I slipped off the bed, put on my clothes, picked my shoes and socks up off the floor. I didn't do the zipper of my jeans because I thought it would make too much of a sound.

"Can't we just ignore him?" Larry Olseth mouthed from the bed. "Won't he just go away?"

Carl pounded the door.

"Give me a minute." Larry Olseth rose from the bed and covered himself with a white bathrobe. As I moved inside the closet, my head nudged a bunch of loose hangers. "Dang," I said, trying to steady about thirty of them with my hand, but they clanged anyway like chimes inside a clock. I pulled the closet door shut from the inside, slowly, to keep the hinges from creaking.

"Now," Carl said, "or I'll blow down the door."

"I'm coming," Larry Olseth said. I heard the lock on the door click and my brother step into the room. The overhead light came on, making shafts inside the closet at my feet, above my head, and through the cracks in the panels. I moved to the far end of the closet and pressed myself against the wall.

"Where's Agnes?" Carl asked. He was scanning the room, taking in the stuff on Larry Olseth's bed and the indentations left by our bodies. I knew he was looking for things of mine in the mess the way he looked for deer droppings on the side of the mountain. "She's been here," he said. "Her smell is here."

"She left hours ago," Larry Olseth said. "She said she was going back to the village."

"I've been to the village," Carl challenged.

"Yeah?" Larry feigned unconcern.

"She wasn't there." He paused. "You two fuck like rabbits, or what?"

Larry Olseth laughed uncomfortably. "This is crazy, Carl."

"So you two think you're leaving tomorrow on the plane?"

It was funny. Larry Olseth was in the bedroom and I was in the closet, but in that instant—the instant when we knew why Carl had come—our heads were as linked to each other as boats in tow. Larry Olseth shook his head and chuckled, but not because anything was humorous. "We were kidding around, Carl. She never said she'd go."

"I heard what she said."

"I've got a girlfriend, Carl. Alice is her name. Alice Wheeler. We've set the date."

"What were you doing with a fifteen-year-old, then?" Carl demanded. I heard the click of the safety and knew then that Carl had brought the deer rifle along with him. But I wasn't worried about Larry Olseth. The gun never had any bullets in it. Besides, it was me Carl wanted, not him.

"So what did you promise her?" Carl asked. "The world?"

"I didn't promise her anything."

"We'll wait for her and see," Carl said. "Tell me a story."

Larry Olseth thought for a moment and said, "Ever hear the one about the sailor?"

"The sailor and the midget?" Carl asked.

"That's a different one," Larry Olseth said. "In this one, he's sitting at supper with his wife and kid."

"Tell it," Carl said.

"The guy's spent his whole life collecting things," Larry Olseth began. "He's done pretty well for himself, trading the junk with the people of the city of Bagdad, where he lives. One day a dervish passes his house and sees the marble pillars and onion domes and thinks to himself, 'Why should he bask in Allah's favor, eat pecans, drink tea from Ceylon, when I'm lucky to get a slice of goat cheese?' The more he thinks about it, the more pissed off he gets. 'I work at least as hard as he does, yet I go hungry while he dines on the brains of monkeys.'"

"Get up," Carl said. I heard the rustle of bedding, the sigh of the mattress, as Larry Olseth stood up. "We're going for a walk." I heard Larry Olseth's feet on the carpet. "Keep talking," Carl said. "You're interesting me." The hinges squeaked as Larry opened the door. Through the wall of the closet, I heard them in the hall. I opened the closet door and crept across the room. I peeked around the jamb as the two boys moved past rooms 11 and 13.

"So the sailor invites the guy in," Larry Olseth continued, "puts him at the head of the table, says, 'Eat.' So the guy eats. The sailor says, 'Perhaps when you've heard my story, you'll think twice before you envy me again.'"

Larry Olseth opened the door to the second-floor landing. "Out." Carl nudged the barrel against the back of Larry's head.

As they moved down the steps, I crept after them, opened the door at the end of the hall and slipped into the night. Their footsteps creaked on the stairs outside like boats against the pier. "'On my first voyage,' says the sailor, 'our captain mistook the back of a sea monster for a small island.'" Larry Olseth stepped onto the sidewalk—a ghost in his white bathrobe, the rifle linking them like a horse and rider. "'Some of us disembarked. Soon the ocean quaked as the island sank beneath our feet. Struggling to keep our heads above water, we watched our ship depart without us.'"

I followed them past the nurse's office, the laundry room, the main desk. The moon was as full as the underbelly of a whale. There were no clouds, no colors, only shades of black and white.

"'Some of us were devoured by the monster. Others by the sea. But by the mercy of waves, a few of us were thrown ashore on the isle of Cassel, once the waiting grounds for grooms of the benevolent maharajah but now the home of the giant, man-eating Cyclops.'"

I stayed in the shadows next to the carpentry shed, crouching behind the concrete blocks stacked next to it, as the boys disappeared behind the machine shop. When I came to the corner, I made myself as long and narrow as a drain spout and poked my head into the walkway.

"She's out there," Carl said. "She's listening." He pushed Larry Olseth past the cannery, the paint supply closet, the scale room, luring me along with the sound of Larry's sweet voice.

"'He scooped us up in his hands the second we arrived and locked us in his cave.'"

They came to a halt in front of the entrance to the butcher line. I followed in the darkness, darting between stacks of pallets.

Carl dropped the key to the garage door on the concrete apron. "Open it," he said. As Larry Olseth picked up the key, I realized he was telling his story to save my life. He thought the longer he kept Carl interested, the more time I would have to go get help. And the truth was, I'd have banged on the door of Windell's cottage, screamed bloody murder to the stars, had I truly believed Larry Olseth was in danger.

The garage door rattled on its runners. "'He looked at each of us. He picked me up by the neck. Then he set me down. I wasn't savory enough for him. He had his eye on our captain.'"

I moved along the outside of the corrugated shed. Lights came on the butcher line, and a thousand tiny rays shot out holes in the metal sheeting. On the other side were the belt, tray tables, and header.

"She's out there," Carl said. "I smell her." I was beside the entrance, next to the block of light, my back pressed against the runner.

"'The Cyclops ran a spit through the head of our captain, then hung him over the fire to cook.'"

From the butcher line came the clank of bolts being loosened.

Larry Olseth saw what I had been trying to tell him all along—that there was nothing Carl wouldn't try if he thought it had the power to frighten. "Louder!" Carl shouted.

"'That night I dreamed of a plan! When the Cyclops asked me my name, I told him it was *Noman!*'"

Carl started up the motor on the header. "She's out there! Tell the story louder!"

The crown began to turn with Larry Olseth collared to it. "'When the Cyclops was fast asleep, I took a spit out of the fire! I climbed his hair! I stood before the huge, closed eye!'"

"Agnes!" Carl screamed.

"'I lifted the hot, orange tip!'"

"Agnes!" he screamed again.

"'And I drove it into the yellow yolk—'"

I stepped into the light as Carl shifted the rotisserie into gear. Behind it, in a convergence of orbits, the blade spun at hundreds of revolutions per second. I walked through the puddles behind the belt. "Agnes," Carl said, shouldering the rifle.

"Agnes!" Larry Olseth screamed, his legs flailing as he came around the other side of the machine, his arms struggling with the spring-loaded collar.

Carl fixed my forehead in the sight. I saw his eye, brown and luminous, on the lens of the scope. As I climbed onto the header platform, I heard the click-click-click of the hammer in the chamber. I knocked the barrel of the rifle aside, and Carl stumbled against the gear shift, knocking it into neutral. Before he could recover, I turned off the switch. Then I picked up the rifle and dropped it down the wooden slide for fish heads.

"You're a whore," Carl said.

"I'm a whore. Right, Carl." I unlocked the collar from around

Larry Olseth's neck. Under his jaw was a red welt that would turn blue on the plane. My boots were inches deep in the slime we hadn't cleaned. I picked a length of intestine from his white robe. "Here," I said and handed it to him. "To practice on." Our eyes met as the slimy piece slipped from his hand onto the floor.

"Don't forget," I said to them both, and I made a little bow, the way Larry Olseth had done to Uma-san, and I left. Someone else could clean up.

THE START OF
SOMETHING

ONE EVENING AT THE END OF A MISERABLE SUMMER IN which neighbor kids bashed down his mailbox a total of thirty-seven times, George Polk told his girlfriend Ellie to move out, to take what she could in her Civic and come back for the rest of her things the next day when he was at work. On a corner of his family's walnut supper table, a tub of margarine liquefied in the heat. On gilt-edged plates lay their cleaned corn cobs, pierced on the ends by porcelain handles. Behind him loomed a dark flowering of his grandfather's firearms, rifles and shotguns George had stuck barrel-first in an umbrella rack brought to America from England in 1843 by his great-great-great-grandfather, George Polk III.

As Ellie began to cry, her hair jerked against the strings of her halter top, tie-dyed orange, red, purple, blue in litmus test spirals. She was twenty-four. He'd been thirty-four for a month. "I don't even know why I love you," she said between sobs. "I don't even know."

An electric fan swept back and forth, no, no, no, no. "You'll be wanting these," he said and handed her an envelope containing the job offers she'd received since publishing the first chapter of her dissertation, "Variations of Wavelength, Frequency, and Temperature of Black Body Radiation." For months they'd arrived at the house from university physics departments in the States and overseas, letters complimenting her work and inviting her to lecture, teach, conduct research in their darkrooms, whatever she wanted, for as long, or as short, a time as she cared to, offering her salaries that made George's stomach seize up like brakes.

She opened the envelope and laughed. "You think I care about these?"

"You ought to care, Ellie," George said, "because opportunities have a way of drying up." A porch light came on across the valley of horse farms, a twinkle far off in the dark silhouette of mountains. He added, "Once you've taken a position somewhere, you'll see I'm right, and you'll be damn glad I forced you out when I did. It'll be as if you're looking down on all this from a great height. You'll see that I saw the truth and you didn't because you were just too young."

Her brows came together on either side of a thin fold. It seemed impossible to him that in her head, between shiny cloves of hair that came to points over shoulders tan from growing pot, there lurked a brilliance harboring all that was known about the phenomenon of light. "Think of it as splitting the atom," he said. "Think of it as fission."

"I've told you a hundred times," she said. "I can't help it if I'm able to comprehend a bunch of stupid scientific jargon. I wish I wasn't able to."

"Don't say that, Ellie."

"Why? Because I sound like you?"

"I'm a defeatist, honey."

"Did you ever think I might be a defeatist, too?"

Her cheeks were as flushed and streaked with tears as they normally were at this stage of the argument, but in her pupils flickered fires that usually burned later, when he slid his hands inside her Levi's and parted the slick flesh between her thighs and looked into her eyes for an assurance that she, who might've developed the first nuclear warhead had she lived forty years earlier, saw in him something equally inexorable and terrifying. As the younger of two fair Protestant daughters, Ellie Gibson would be endowed by the old money of her Richmond parents if she chose never again to set foot in a physics lab, while he had nothing but the certainty that no one as successful as she could be satisfied for long with a failure like him. She knelt on the floor beside him and, pressing her face against his side, toyed with his belt loops.

"The university never hires its own graduate students," she said, "but that doesn't mean I can't teach at Rand Moore, or one of the junior colleges, or even one of the high schools."

Her arm lay on his lap like a boomerang. In her hair he smelled the weed she'd smoked on the drive home from the university, her Mardi Gras beads and feathered roach clips jiggling from the rearview mirror as the estates and hay fields of the newly rich passed by outside. "Jesus, Ellie," he said, "how many times do we have to mull over this before you pick up and leave?"

She unbuckled his belt and zipped open his fly, and as his penis rose from the slit in his underwear, he eased onto the back legs of his chair, watched her lips cover the tip of him, her hair flutter over him. He withdrew a Civil War-era Colt .30-30 from the rack behind him, held the carbine over his head with both hands, thumbs locked around the trigger, the barrel a straight shaft to the part in her hair, a thin pink line that rose and fell on wings like the spine of a dove. When he came, she looked up into the bore, and he saw fear cross her face like the shadow of a cloud as his spurting cock slithered from her mouth and lay, distended, on his clothed thigh.

"You're not going to kill me, are you, George?" she asked, backing across the floor on all fours. He shouldered the rifle and peered past the front and rear sights at her perfect forehead, inside which lay the sea. He clicked out the safety. "Sweet Jesus," she said, "please don't kill me, George."

She wiped her mouth with the back of her wrist, and he buckled himself and told her to get up off the floor and turn around slowly. "I don't want to see you again, understand?" he said. "I want to read about you from here on out."

He placed her job offers in her hand, and she glanced over her shoulder at him—as if the caring at the heart of a cruel and absurd statement were a doorknob she could turn—and saw the dark muzzle of his rifle aimed at her brain. As she walked toward the door, he followed her through the columns of furniture he'd inherited from the house on Marshall Street in Richmond—rockers stacked on top of love seats on top of sofas, buffet tables stacked on top of vanities on top of chests-of-drawers, and grandfather clocks, thirteen in all, the crests and finials of which peeked above columns of shipping crates and slip-covered easy chairs—to the stoop. Nine o'clock, and outside the leaves were streaked with moonlight. They walked through the caskets of light that lay across the lumber and pipe left over from building his house when chimes sounded through the door behind them in a stentorian clangor that set his hound, Burgreen, howling at the stars. Below in the valley, Jack

Heston's black lab, Lady, howled in reply, and soon dogs at the base of the Blue Ridge were howling too.

Ellie's car was parked beside his truck on the hard earth to the left of Burgreen's pen. She opened the car door and closed it quickly behind her, and George stood before the grille pointing the rifle at an apparition that shimmered on her windshield like a doily under water. He thought it was her face, but when he squinted to make out the sockets of her eyes, the pink of her lips, he saw that it was only the moon, broken into strands by the trees. When her headlights came on, he stood at the center of an orb of brightness.

"You won't see me again, George." Her voice sounded tinny and detached. "Because, so help me God, this is the last time I'm driving down this lumpy goddamn road of yours. You can do what you want with my things. Burn them. Bury them. I don't want them anymore."

"Okay," he said.

"This is a vet thing, isn't it?" she said at last.

"No," he said. "It isn't a vet thing."

She jerked the car into reverse and backed behind the trunk of a black walnut tree. He sat down on a carpet of pine needles and set the rifle beside him and watched her taillights double-u down a drive he'd cleared with a chainsaw and a rental bulldozer. To his right, Burgreen whimpered through the chain links. Below him spanned a firmament of lit windows and barn lights, and as he lay his head against a slope of earth, he heard the twenty-six distinctive ticks and tocks inside the house and imagined the clockworks were gears the size of mill wheels, and he was floating on a millstream under a still night sky, blanketed above and below by stars. When the chimes sounded the quarter hour, he went back inside the house, fit the rifle into its slot in the rack, cleared the table of dishes, washed them in the sink, and put them away in a corniced china cabinet with doors of arched-top glass and a domed shell of New England scrimshaw.

Ellie hadn't kept much at the house. His father, a chain-smoking army chaplain, had died the year before of lung cancer, and although the house George'd built was an eighth the size of the family's old tobacco manor, he'd filled it with all but an 18 x 36 U-Store-It locker of his family's most prized heirlooms. From Ellie's closet in the upstairs bedroom he withdrew armloads of her clothes, mostly jeans and thread-bare trousers and wool sweaters and flannel shirts, but a few dresses that tumbled coolly as creek water over his forearms, and carried them out to the truck. He emptied drawers of her socks, cutoffs, tank tops, under-wear, and miscellaneous beadwork and jewelry into plastic garbage bags. When the bags were full he carried them to the truck as well. He ripped her Humidity-Lamps and Gro-Tanks from the wall and threw them, pot sprouts and all, in with the kitchen trash. From the attic he retrieved six boxes of her books and the king-sized futon they'd slept on when the house was little more than a foundation and frame on the side of a mountain. When he'd heaped these on top of her clothes, he tied everything down with ropes. Then he turned off every light in the house but one and unplugged the fan.

Outside, he started his truck and inched through the woods down the boulder-laden zigzag of a drive, seeing the red of Ellie's taillights as if she were right in front of him, as if she hadn't left hours ago. On the winding rural route through North Garden, he cranked open the window to feel the illusion of wind, and into the cab came the smell of cut grass and the scream of cicadas. He lit a smoke. Outside the After Hours Supper Club and Lounge he saw the van of his roofing partner Ed. Customizing the rear doors, a pit viper clutched in a bald eagle's talons. He slowed, but kept driving, over the dry rock beds of Horseshoe Creek and Rockfish Creek, through the crossroads of North Garden proper, to the sign for Rand Moore Women's College, established in 1869. He parked in a visitor lot, between a BMW and an Audi, and when the night watchman's flashlight glinted through the mimosas, he ducked below the steering column till the man's shoe-clops faded behind the chapel. Then he went on foot, under a cover of weeping willows, past the science center and student union to a sidewalk that wound past the new power plant to the riding stables. He crossed it, cut up between dormitories, over a shuffleboard court, and through a hedge of azalea bushes surrounding the president's courtyard, to the bluff where the abandoned plant sat, the one with the cherry-tipped smokestack he could see from his house.

He'd scaled the smokestack plenty of times. A narrow ladder was bolted every six and a half feet to the bricks, and on a night as cloudless as this one, he'd be able to see a Jeffersonian dome of whiteness over Charlottesville, as well as lights from homes nestled into the James River Valley clear to Lynchburg. As he climbed, he felt the coolness of the rungs in his hands, the beads of dew the still air laid on his bare shoulders, and the vertigo that came with rising above the dark crowns of tall trees. Sometimes, as he sat with his legs across the dark opening, a college girl led her boyfriend across the clearing and disappeared into bogs and scrub brush the college leased to a Richmond hunting club. Sometimes they made it only to the clearing before they pulled each other to the earth, and if he looked down, he could see them below in the dirt, climbing on top of each other like beetles. Once, having heard the high-pitched voices of two women, he'd descended the ladder to within a few feet of girls lying side by side on a bedding of blankets, and he'd watched their hands pass as gently as breezes through each other's clothes. But tonight there was no rustling of fabrics, no snapping of twigs, no laughter or crying. Across a valley of stars, the neon tube above his sink flickered through the trees and, below in a dimly lit parking lot, sat his four-wheel drive, laden with Ellie's things. What in the world he would do with the stuff he hadn't a clue, but at least he had the space he needed to store the rest of his inheritance. From his pants pocket he removed his truck keys, held them between his knees over the hole, and let them fall freely into the darkness. Then he applied the treads of his boots to the inside of the smokestack and dipped into the mouth, his thighs to his chest, his back hard against the bricks, and as he started down after his keys he felt the pull in his stomach of the distance below him.

A WEEK PASSED, AND STILL GEORGE WOKE UP ANGRY, THE SUN bearing down on him through his bedroom window. From the kitchen he saw his bashed-in mailbox lying on the road where it had stayed three days running, the flag a spot of red on Jack Heston's perfectly mowed bluegrass. Out in his pen, Burgreen was humping the fence again, barking his damn head off. He set his coffee down, pulled a rifle from the umbrella rack behind him, moved the scope over the golf-course-green hills of Burnley Estate and Farm till the crosshairs fell on Jack Heston's lab, Lady. Each of Burgreen's barks was answered by one of hers, and so, he told himself, the time had come to put an end to the madness. He squeezed the trigger as the blue-black dog circled between the paddock and stables. Then he moved the scope across the buggy track, tack shop, and narrow wading pool for horses, to the house, traced a fluted column to a window on the second story where, between taffeta curtains kept apart by tie-backs, Jack Heston combed his glistening gray hair. George squeezed the trigger again and aimed the rifle at the flashing red signal on the smokestack at Rand Moore Women's College.

The dogs still barked at one another, Jack Heston put down his comb and buttoned his dress shirt. George set the firearm on the table, and the smudges his elbows left on the surface shrank into themselves and vanished. "See, the gun wasn't loaded, Ellie," he said. "None of them are. I'll show you, honey."

He opened the chambers of a double-barreled 12-gauge shotgun, ejected the clip of a .30-06 hunting rifle, dismantled one weapon after another till all but the Colt .30-30 he'd put to her head lay in a heap before him. He picked up this rifle by the small of its stock, and when he marshaled the bolt across the breach, a bullet flicked from the magazine onto the tabletop. He marshaled it again, and a second shell flicked out, and then a third. He held his face and wept.

After awhile he phoned up friends of his, guys he'd known before he met Ellie, but those who were home were on their way to a rock band rehearsal, a Harley-Davidson auction, a daughter's field hockey game. When he told his friends who was calling, they said they were glad to hear from him, but he couldn't tell them about Ellie, about how he'd nearly blown out her brains, not on a Saturday after a year and a half of silence. So he made plans for drinks and catching up, plans, he knew, that would never materialize, and phoned his partner Ed.

"Sons of bitches bashed down my mailbox again."

"You called to tell me that?" Ed asked.

"I called because I'm building a new mailbox, and I guess I was hoping you'd lend me a hand."

"What are you building it out of?" Ed asked.

"Septic pipe. Pre-PVC. Swear to god it's heavy as a goddamn tank barrel."

"Unh-hunh," Ed said.

"Once I get it in the ground," George said, "I reckon I'll have the only indestructible mailbox in the county. Let's see those goddamn kids take this one out."

"Indestructible?"

"Tune a juvenile delinquent's bones to high C," George said. "Send a $40,000 automobile into a tailspin, maybe into an oak."

"Sure, George, I'll lend you a hand."

"Really?" said George. "Well, that's just fine. I'll see you in an hour then." As he hung up the phone, George felt giddy. This time he wasn't going to squander his money on a new mailbox, and he wasn't going to waste his time repairing an old.

Below on the Hestons' property, workers had set up cardtables and folding chairs underneath a blue and white striped tent. George put on some old clothes and a pair of boots and hauled his tanks of oxygen and acetylene, his torch, eye shields, and asbestos gloves up from the cellar onto the lawn. As a lieutenant in the Army Corp of Engineers stationed outside a burning Kuwait City, he'd repaired armor-plated amphibious vehicles when they returned from missions on the deserts south of An-Nafud. Like his father, a Presbyterian minister who'd enlisted during the Korean War and spent Vietnam preaching to GIs on U.S. installations in western Europe, he'd thought of the army as a woman, rife with opportunities for the man who treated her right, and though he'd acquired a bag of skills in a two-year tour of duty in which mines, mortars, and machine-gun fire were virtually nonexistent, he no longer believed a woman rife with anything save the needs of any person, and he thought of the army in this way too.

With an oxyacetylene flame he heated pipe until his drag-line turned liquidy and orange, then he squeezed the handle on the oxygen jet till a kerf appeared in the puddle, a fissure flanked by bubbling metal. He cut two sections, a ten footer and a three, and joined them at right angles to each other. From the steel he'd removed from the joint, he fashioned a door, firing it till it was soft, then flattening it on an anvil. He attached it to the box by a hinge, and as his welds cooled, he loaded a post-hole digger, wheelbarrow, and two fifty-pound sacks of concrete into his truck bed. As he worked he hardly thought about Ellie, and he told her so.

"Keep busy is the key," he said. "Don't think," he said. "Do," he said. "Be."

Ed appeared at the top of the drive just as George finished painting the K in POLK. A vet in his fifties, his sandy locks pulled into a tight ponytail and a day pack slung across one shoulder, Ed wore dungarees and a T-shirt the same blue as George's newly painted letters, sleeves rolled up over rounded, powerful arms. George waved him over to the mailbox.

"What do you think?" he asked. The welds looked so solid George couldn't imagine their cracking under the heaviest pressure.

"A person crazy enough to swing a bat at that thing would splinter his arms," Ed said, squinting through wire-rim spectacles at the black monolithic L lying on the parched lawn.

George tapped down the lid on the can of paint. "I only want to put an end to this nonsense," he declared and flossed out a bit of gristle from between his teeth with a stalk of dead grass.

"Guess I'd be surprised if you put an end to it," Ed said, laughter lines cutting into his cheeks in deep, crescent-shaped trenches.

"What're you getting at, Ed?"

"Getting at what I see in front of me," Ed said.

"And what's that?"

"A challenge." Ed spit. "One look, and I'd be back with explosives."

"Well, I guess that's just you." George stood up and walked toward the truck as Ed removed his day pack carefully from his shoulder, opened it ceremoniously, and palmed a flesh-colored bomb the size of a baseball.

"See this?" Ed called. "It's made from ammonium nitrate, potassium bichromate, and naphthalene. Compounds I extracted myself from mothballs, saltpeter, ammonia, and tanner's alum."

"So," George hollered back.

"I'm talking ordinary household products," Ed went on. "Products any kid could find in his home."

"You call tanner's alum an ordinary household product?"

"Round here it is."

George came to look at the bomb up close. Except for the wires, it might have been a wad of the same stuff he'd played with as a little kid, a German version of Silly-Putty called *Zuper-Putti*, with baby angels on the plastic egg it came in.

"Made my first when I was fourteen," Ed said.

George crossed his arms. "You're full of shit if you think that's going to put the tiniest dent in my mailbox."

Ed grew somber, meditative—as he did whenever they hit upon the subject of bombs. "It might not," he admitted. "But you're never going to know if we don't test it."

"We're not testing anything," George said.

Below on the Hestons' property, a four-piece New Orleans-style brass band practiced a number, the drones of a trombone, sousaphone, and trumpet rising on the beat of drums through a swish of tree limbs. A breeze, the first in weeks, cooled George's forehead. "Got anything to drink?" Ed asked.

"Well water."

"Is it potable?"

"There's a full bar inside. I could make us what they're having down at the Hestons'."

"And what's that?" Ed asked.

"Mint juleps I reckon," George said.

"We play croquet, too?"

"Croquet, lawn darts, you name it," George said, "soon as we get my mailbox in the ground."

"Naw," Ed said. "If we played croquet they'd have to fish your ball out of the wedding punch down there. I'd send you flying off the mountain."

"Wedding punch? Someone getting married?"

Ed raised his eyebrows, grinning. "It was only announced in the papers three Sundays in a row. Tenille Heston? Jack Heston's daughter. Dark hair. Pouty face. Sorta mean looking."

"Her? I've seen her racing past me on my way to work. She must be all of twenty."

"That'd be her."

"A gorgeous blur," George said. "That's what she's been to me."

"Well hell," said Ed, "she won't sit down in a vehicle unless it's a Porsche or Audi."

"I had no idea she lived down there," George said. "Every time I've seen her she's had a look of such discontent on her face. I wanted to tell her, 'Hell, girl, things can't be that bad.'"

"Well, she's marrying Bertram Deutsch of Deutsch Motors now. He'll give her everything her daddy gave her and more. Which is more than you or I could give her if we won the goddamn lottery."

George shook his head, grabbed a clump of mint leaves from the patch of herbs Ellie had planted beside the house. "Funny," he said, "I've never once seen her down there."

"Been looking, have you?" Ed asked.

"Jesus, Ed, they're what I see when I look out my window. I wish they weren't there. I wish the whole valley weren't there. Then maybe I wouldn't have to waste my time on mailboxes."

Ed laughed. "Well, it's not like you'll be getting any. Now that Ellie's gone."

George had the mint leaves steeping in sugar water before he understood Ed meant mail. From inside the house he watched Ed bend down and open the lid of the mailbox and press the explosive inside it. "I told you," George shouted through the kitchen window, "I don't want you setting off bombs on my property." Ed hummed "Raindrops" as he unspooled fuse across the lawn. Through the screen door, George watched him connect the wires to a light switch he'd removed from his pack, the switch itself connected by wires to a fourteen-volt dry-cell battery. When the drinks were ready, George carried them out to the porch and set them on the picnic table.

"Which do you suppose we're testing?" Ed asked. "The mailbox or the bomb?"

"Neither," George said.

With a twitch of his hand Ed completed the circuit. A thunderous fountain of flame erupted over the roof and trees, a pillar a foot thick and twenty feet high. "Goddamn it!" Not believing even Ed would do this, George had to admit it was a spectacular sight.

Ed saluted to shield his eyes. "Are we not living in the best of all possible worlds?" he asked solemnly.

George knew the ashes he was seeing weren't devils, but the harder he squinted, the more defined they became, like bees isolated in a swarm. They were red, with triangular, black widow's peaks combed neatly between their horns, and as they flew on pitchforks around and around the radiant shaft, their tails undulated behind them like serpents. Gaining speed, some were cast from their orbits by their own momentum, and as they fizzled, he saw the tiny, malicious grins change into slack-jawed confusion and horror. Others lit on the grass and in trees, setting them ablaze. Soon dozens of small fires crackled on the lawn and in branches and in the underbrush of the encroaching woods.

"Guess we better put out the fires," Ed said, the eruption collapsing back into the mailbox, the devils vanishing into the hot air. George felt the same implacable tiredness he always felt. His friends, those that there were, had families. He had Ed, and as the sad truth of this closed around him like the smoke of a he attached a hose to the spigot and began spraying out what fires he could.

In the woods fins of smoke coursed up from the ferns and ivy and, a little way up from the house, fire coiled around a dead limb of an oak. As the limb cracked off from the trunk, torches leapt from the ground cover, flicking fire onto the yellow leaves of small maples and the dead underboughs of pines. He could never put out all the fires, this he quickly saw. The hose was only fifty feet long and the flames had already spread beyond Ellie's pot plants into the clearing where power lines sagged past the house down to the road.

Ed stashed the spool underneath the deck with the detonating equipment as sirens sounded in the distance. "You pissed at me?" Ed asked.

"No, I ain't pissed at you." Though George couldn't have said why.

In no time wedding guests began to assemble at the top of the drive to watch the fire, jabbering in excited voices about wind directions and where the fires would spread if they weren't put out quickly. Route 6. Fulsome's Garage. Morris's Fruit Stand. "It's a shame," George heard someone say. "There's nothing but more helpless poor folks living on the other side of Reynold's Mountain, and Lord knows they aren't equipped over there to handle a fire." More guests ascended through the trees, men in tuxedos and women in long sleeveless dresses, carrying cocktails and hors d'oeuvres on white napkins, and it surprised and impressed George that these people, as wealthy as they were, knew what lay beyond their own two- and three-hundred acre spreads. He didn't want them there—they were trespassing on his land and invading his privacy—and yet, having never seen them save in the society pages of the local paper or as they sped past in expensive imports, he was fascinated by their faces, by how the corners of Mary Harris's mouth turned down when she laughed and how Sam Merchantson's nose was even larger and more rounded than it appeared in photos.

Ed handed him his mint julep and stood beside him as water flooded the lawn. Soon a ragtag team of county firefighters unrolled a doughnut wheel past Burgreen's pen, and the dog twitched an ear. In spite of the commotion, Burgreen lay asleep in the dirt, his paws extended fore and aft. When the firemen reached the end of a hose, another was connected to it, and soon they were in the forest above the property, gone save for the snapping of twigs and the clipped broadcasts of walkie-talkies. As quickly as the fires had started, they had left, pushing on, and a thick bank of smoke moved in front of the sun, making the air jaundiced and heavy. In the woods three teenage boys in sport coats darted stealthily between the trees. When the water came on, it surged through the flaccid canvas and erupted in a mushroom cap of yellow steam. The people applauded, and George wished he'd set his house on fire. How they'd clap at the sight of his clocks collapsing into themselves and at the cacophony of chimes.

"I was wondering something about you," Ed said, gazing up the mountain at what might have been a volcano about to blow. "About why you never get angry or depressed. We're a lot alike that way. I never get angry or depressed either. But I used to, and sometimes I miss it."

"What are you talking about, Ed? Far as I'm concerned, you're a goddamned guru."

"When I was a kid," Ed said, "back in the fifties, my eyes used to put wings on everything. Say I found a black widow spider sitting on a sac of eggs, that spider would have long, horsefly wings. Or if I came across a poisonous snake in a field somewhere, it would have wings like a hawk. Even my ma and pa had wings. Theirs were large and fleshy, and usually they kept them hidden under their clothes, but if I went out walking by myself in the fields, I'd see them in the sky hovering like condors. At night I'd see their faces outside my bedroom window. You have any idea what a frightening place the world is when everything that means you harm has wings?"

George had noticed Ed's peculiarities, how he'd filled a cassette with "Raindrops" and, when the other workers yelled at him to turn it off, came to the job site with a Walkman fastened to his tool belt. "My aunt was the one person who understood it. One evening she sat me down in a chair in front of the stove and told me to put my head back and gaze down into the orange coals. Soon I was very relaxed. Maybe I was even hypnotized, I don't know. What I remember is my aunt standing over me with knitting needles, and the steam rising from them as the warm steel went into my head through my eye sockets." Ed laughed. "My aunt knew what she was doing, though she was forty-seven years old and hadn't advanced beyond grade six."

"She messed with your brains?" George asked. "Is that what you're telling me?"

"I don't know what she did. But it worked. Only bats and birds and insects had wings, and nothing angered or depressed me after that."

As water from the firemen's hoses coursed back through the trees in chutes of froth, a helicopter edged toward the fire's nexus, dispensing flame-retardant chemicals. "It was about the best thing that ever happened to me," Ed went on above the what-what-what of rotor blades. "Why I was able to survive three years in a bamboo cage in the mountains north of Chi-chu while other POWs were seeing their mothers, girlfriends, and wives in the clouds, in the heads of farm animals, in the smiles and winks of their torturers."

The backflow from the firemen's hoses turned pink with retardant as the helicopter dropped behind the mountain. "I'd never go back," Ed said. "Mean I'd never have what she did reversed, if that's even possible. But sometimes I wonder if I wasn't made a little less human."

George didn't want to hear about brains being messed with,

not with his neighbors standing around as if on safari, and the thick spray through the woods of the firemen returning. What had happened today was embarrassing. "Truth is," Ed said, "I sometimes wonder if your brains haven't been messed with."

"Right," George said.

"Well, have they?"

"Not with knitting needles."

"Then why don't you go up to Tenille Heston and kiss her on the mouth?" Ed asked.

"Jesus," George said. "What the hell does that have to do with it?" He kicked the ground, and a sodden divot of earth and grass splashed in a puddle. "It's got everything to do with it," said Ed. "You want to teach these people a lesson about respecting other people's property—if that's what you're feeling—then go on up to the sweetest piece of property they possess and besmirch it, just once, with your lips."

George looked at Tenille Heston standing in a white chiffon wedding dress beside her father, her hair hidden by a plumed Gainsborough hat tilted across one eye, what few hardnesses there were to her face softened by a veil and makeup. "I dare you," said Ed, taking the hose from George's hand as firemen moved across the yard as methodically as fumigators and, with gushes of water from a heavy brass nozzle, removed the candlelight flickers from between the sheets of standing water.

"The wedding's been spoiled," cried Mary Harris in a shrill voice that rose from the heart of the congregation and fell like soot onto the shoulders and heads of the onlookers. Now that the fires were out, men straightened their lapels, women primped themselves in vanity mirrors removed from pastel handbags.

"I'm not kissing anyone," George declared and turned to look at the fireman who stood beside him in black boots, helmet, and turn-out.

"This is going to cost you," said the fireman. "This is going to cost you plenty."

"What do you mean?" said George. "The fire was the result of a welding accident. A spark from my goddamn welding torch started all this." He waved his arms, and the fireman smiled knowingly.

"Two eyewitnesses say you boys lit off more than a Tennessee salute."

"Two eyewitnesses?"

"Couple kids digging for treasure in yonder woods prit near described the apocalypse," said the fireman.

NOW GEORGE WAS BY HIMSELF INSIDE THE HOUSE, LISTENING to Burgreen's barking. How the dog could sleep through an explosion and sirens, then wake to the chirping of crickets, was beyond him. Indeed he'd have put the psychotic animal out of its misery long ago had he not been fearful of nighttime sleep himself. On the kitchen table rested his guns, and he thought how in the moonlight they looked like bones, and he thought of the bones he had seen as a fifteen-year-old kid traveling with his father in Europe. His father had taken him out of school for an autumn vacation, and together they'd driven to Munich for Oktoberfest, then across the Austrian border to Altmunster-an-der-Traunsee, a city of whitewashed cafes and inns pressed between Alps and a chasm of the bluest water he had ever seen. His father and he sat on a veranda overlooking the lake and the sailboats and the fly fishermen casting below from the rocks. On a white linen tablecloth stood two liters of the local beer, and a walnut torte to share, for his father believed sampling a region's delicacies an essential part of a practical education.

Across the street was a small stone church, which his father gave him fifty pfennigs to go inside and see. As he crossed to it, he saw the row of stained glass windows along one side, with cinquefoils and quatrefoils and depictions of such biblical stories as Jesus among the lepers and the resurrection of Lazarus. Inside the doors sat an old woman with crippled legs, and on her lap, a gold alms basin with red felt lining. He placed the coins on the felt and stepped inside the church proper. The nave, lit by three altar candles, was much narrower than he expected, with six wooden pews, each wide enough to fit three thin congregants. Then he saw that each had been sawed off on the sides to make room for the bones, ulnae and radii, fibulae, femurs, and ribs, disconnected and stacked like sticks against the walls and behind the cross, neatly, so as to conserve space. Vertebrae occupied one corner, as did bones of the feet and hands, carefully collected and kept in place with chicken wire. In another corner rose the skulls, maxillae on top of parietals in totems that touched the ceiling, and behind each pair of gaping sphenoids, someone, perhaps the crippled lady, had set the mandibles of the lower jaw.

He liked being in the church. The bones were clean and, organized as they were by type, lent an atmosphere of timelessness and calm missing from the Quonset huts in which his father preached. He sat down in a pew and entered the most intricate dream of himself he'd had until then. He saw the woman who would become his wife—she bore his mother's name, Ellen—the son they would have—George Polk IX—their dog, Cooter, their cat, Barbara Bane, and even their car, a lime '57 Fairlane. When his father came for him an hour later and, smelling of cigarette smoke and beer, whispered from the pew behind him, "'For it is a day of trouble, and of treading down, and of perplexity by the Lord God of hosts in the valley of vision.' Isaiah twenty-two, verse five," he understood why his father had sent him to the reliquary, and the peace within him was confirmed.

That none of his dream had come to pass hardly mattered now, for his father was dead. What troubled him was that he had ever looked at human bones and not seen the bodies from which they came. For even as he looked at his guns and saw bones, they were the bones of people who had lived, bones that protruded from sleeves and pant legs, bones that were still warm. His grandfather clocks ticked and tocked. In a week he had succeeded in utilizing every square foot of space in the house that he lacked the finances to finish, stacking his family's possessions on the stairs and in the attic, in the halls and closets and the area around his bed, so that to get to the bathroom, to get to his chest of drawers, to get to clocks in need of winding, he had to move as if through a maze. Most nights he could not stay there.

AT THE BOTTOM OF HIS DRIVE, HE STOPPED HIS TRUCK. Across the road, Tenille Heston stood in a vertex of spotlight beams, her leg raised on a balcony railing, the white train of her wedding dress dangling onto yew bushes. Her husband, a generation removed from her in age, sat behind her on a canopied bed while, below on the lawn, a dozen well-groomed boys and men waited for her garter. George drove on, past trees lit by fireflies and ponds awash with moonlight. A mile before the sign for Rand Moore Women's College, he turned onto hunting club land and followed two winding ruts he'd discovered only that week, past deer stands that rose from the gray brush like prison sentries and pearl-eyed jackrabbits that darted out from under the transfixing rays of his headlights. He left the vehicle in a blind of redbud and pin oak and, when he heard no sound but the scurrying of field mice, he walked across the clearing to the abandoned power plant.

Once, before his house had a roof much less electricity, he'd brought Ellie to the top of the smokestack. He'd made sure her back rested against the signal's sturdy casing, and when she was as comfortable as she was ever going to be perched above the earth with her legs dangling into the chasm, he produced two wine glasses and a bottle of Grands-Echezeaux 1961 from his father's cellar. It was autumn, and as they drank she showed him the constellations of Cepheus, Cassiopeia, and their child Andromeda, then pointed at the mountain where he'd broken ground less than a month before. "Can you guess the name of that one?" she asked. "The brightest constellation of them all?"

Not even the last dying embers of their campfire glowed in the direction she pointed. "Home," she said. When the wine was gone, she dropped bottle and glasses both into the hole, said, "Shhh," for a kerplink that never came. He thought about that on nights when she stayed late at the darkroom and he waited over the shaft for a window to light up across the way, how not the faintest tinkle had emerged as a report. So he had filled his pockets with stones and small change, a backpack with bottles and jars, which he dropped, a piece at a time, into the blackness of the smokestack. Once he brought up a kafir lily from his father's funeral and dropped it, pot and all, into the opening. Once he brought up glass Javanese fishing floats, which he'd bought in Singapore for a hundred dollars each, and dropped them both into darkness, but it had been as if he sat atop a pillar of silence.

Then, a week ago, in far worse shape than he was now, he'd let his truck keys fall into the smokestack. By then Ellie was as gone as if he'd heaved her himself into the abyss, and he hadn't been sure he wanted to go on living. He'd applied his boot treads to the inside of the smokestack and dipped into the mouth, his knees to his chest, his back hard against the cement. To have forced Ellie from the house at gunpoint was to insure that she would never come back, but to have allowed her to stay would have been to capitulate to the weakest part of her nature. As his head had gone below the lip, he'd smelled soot. If he kept his legs stiff and did not allow himself to become too comfortable, he'd found he could lower himself into the smokestack. He'd taken the appropriate measure, of this he'd been convinced, for Ellie would not have left through sane discourse. And this, the impossibility of knowing beforehand the force needed to achieve a result, had seemed to him the truth at the crux of life itself. He'd inched deeper into the blackness, till the opening to the sky and stars had appeared no larger than a salad plate. Perhaps he would kill himself, just retract his limbs and plummet, but as he'd moved like a spider downward into the cavity, his muscles extended and flexed as if intent upon their own survival. He'd thought of his guns, how much easier everything would be without them, although he knew he would never part with them, just as he would never part with a single one of his family's possessions. Indeed, he'd enjoyed thinking of them there in his house on a mountain somewhere in the world. And he'd thought of Ellie, how she, too, was in the world, as his knees had drawn farther away with each minute descension, and fatigue in fingers and toes had crept into arms and legs the longer he'd made them. The smokestack had not been a straight shaft, but one that flared as it went down, and although he'd had no idea how far down he'd traveled, the way out seemed as distant as the planets. He'd rolled his eyeballs back, stared upward like a man coursing through space on a saucer, and as the exit narrowed to a point of darkness, the pain in his feet, neck, and hands took on the colors of bricks, wood, and sky, and he'd been spinning. And then he'd lain on a surface of stones and glass and pot shards, his body as rigid as if it had been an inch off of the floor.

That was a week ago. Now Ellie's futon cushioned him when he reached the bottom. It climbed the walls like cell-padding. Here, among clothes and books he'd carried to the top of the smokestack and lowered in with ropes, he would think of things that did not concern him and thereby make himself well. He set a candle on his chest, lit the wick, and as wings of light enfolded him, regret and fear twined themselves into a single thread of smoke. Here, he would spend the nights he did not drink. Here, he would set up a slanty roof of tin to channel rainwater onto the floor of the boiler room. He'd cut a hole in it, run a vent through it, and when winter set in, he'd warm himself with fire.

ICE BREAKING

Sy Johnson trudged onto the frozen lake toting the dismembered body of his lover on a red plastic sled. He walked perhaps two hundred feet, then turned to look at the gold Mustang he had driven north from Isabella and parked on the public landing. Its grille was rusted and caked with brown snow. With its left headlight busted and dangling from the wires, it looked a sad piece of machinery. To his Auntie Barto, when she came looking for him, the car would be a prelude to terror—like a torn scrap of shirt on the trail to a scene of bloodshed. Already she had seen that her fifty pounds of birdseed wasn't in the spot where she'd told him to deliver it, behind the porch swing between the cedar planters. Perhaps at this moment she was shaking the shoulders of her neighbor, old Heck Miller, and swiveling his hairless, arthritic legs off the bed. To Wallace Triangle, whose fine white body lay in four parts in a gunnysack on the sled, whose own fingers had tied the piece of rope which supported the Mustang's muffler and pipes, the car had always been a source of joy. But then, Wallace Triangle took joy in sad things.

On the southern horizon, light poured from the slit of moon onto the snow and ice. Soon it would be daybreak. Across the frozen bay rested the island he and Wallace named Baskatong Hump because its high cliffs were shaped like tongs and in the summer, when the northerns and walleyes slowed in the afternoon, they had basked on the exposed rocks above the lake and their beached canoe. Now the island blended with the strip of shoreline and the sky. Yet Sy had walked with Wallace across the ice to the tiny fishing shack so many winter nights, he could have felt his way using only the ice pick. From time to time the red plastic sled caught on the snow, and Sy yanked the cord until Wallace, the styrofoam bucket of minnows, and the four Fish-N-Flags skimmed smoothly again at his side.

"Wallace Triangle," he said, "you remember once telling me that anyone could be made to buy any product, provided he had the liquid assets to make the purchase?"

He'd met Wallace in Finland, Minnesota, at the Baptism River Bar in 1983. At the same bar in the same booth one year later, Wallace had told him about his scheme to unload five thousand inflatable decoy geese. The gunnysack rolled a little on the sled as if to say, *My mind's grown feeble, Sy, you've got to help me now to remember.* "We were drinking stingers, Wallace, your drink. You said, so long as the need is made known."

"That's what I said, Sy, and for a number of years now, we've lived a tidy life."

Sy nodded. They'd unloaded all but three hundred of the semi-durable vinyl geese, each with its own twenty-five ounce steel sinker, in less than two weeks. Those that remained, Sy had peddled to members of his immediate family, which spanned the region from Lax Lake to Cass Lake north to Kabetogama. With the profits, they'd repossessed the fishing shack which had once belonged to his brother, Dean, and had even used it as an office for a time, until, unloading an assortment of plastic lawn ornaments, they'd had the capital to buy up a small warehouse in Isabella. This they had filled with birdseed of the highest quality, in sacks ranging from five pounds to fifty, and had even made a name for themselves, Johnson-Triangle Birdseed Outlet.

"But what you don't understand, what I lacked the heart to tell you, Wallace, is that the only need we ever made known was our own. Our customers were every last one of them family. My family, Wallace. Johnson blood. That's what kept us afloat, and it's a fact I feel ashamed. I do and I know it."

The gunnysack rode easily on the sled, Wallace's legs, torso, and head having settled finally into the jerk and glide of Sy's pace over the frozen lake. The fact was he could not visit a single relative's house for supper without confronting a half dozen of the smiling green and yellow turtles, the frogs with tongues in full extension, the elfin toadstools and grazing deer, all of them cast out of a shiny synthetic that would outlast the people who owned them by thousands of years. Worse was finding his stock still on the racks of small retail outlets. Family, themselves the struggling owners of bait shops and groceries, laundromats and hardware stores, had, in kindness and love, taken on merchandise that hadn't moved in years and wouldn't till they took it home themselves.

"No, Sy," came Wallace's voice from the silhouette of pine tops and across the ice in an eerie gust, "we beautified."

"That may be easy for you to say."

"You're forgetting, Sy, about the sunflower seeds and suet, our stock for the last eighteen months."

"Good acts don't cancel bad ones. You should know that."

"But the good ones count for something. Think of the white-throated sparrow, the yellow-billed cuckoo, the black-throated blue warbler. Think of your grandmother Fern."

"You've never seen a brown-headed cowbird perched on one of our fourteen-foot plastic windmills."

"There's beauty in that."

"That's not a sight you'll have to live with. And if you think I'm going to, Wallace—"

"*Both* of us will, Sy. That's the beauty."

In a lagoon of the island he and Wallace had planted the four cinder blocks on which the tiny four-hole fishing shack rested over the ice. The sun had not yet risen, but its legs streaked upward into starry space like the blood splashes of a creature pulverized in a single blow of god Kawishiwi's stone mallet. Four hundred feet from shore sat the shack, a toolshed really, the scarred remains of a house that had been. Its walls of asbestos and ceiling of tin had withstood the flames of arson as well as any chimney—the winter night Dean took himself, Sara, and their two boys out of the world. Sy pulled the sled up to the rickety plywood door. Behind the shack he opened the valve on the tank of propane, then he picked up the gunnysack and carried Wallace inside.

"You cold?" Sy asked.

"Cold?" the gunnysack replied. In the cupboard above the sink Sy found the box of matches where he and Wallace had left it less than a week before, nestled among kitchen utensils, old invoices, tools, and scraps of tackle. The stove lit, he took the crowbar from the cupboard, removed the entangled confusion of bobbers and fishing line from its neck, and applied its head to a plank in the floor. As he pushed down on the forked end, the board reared up, making an opening fanged like a snake's mouth. He gripped the board between four rust-encrusted nails and pried it loose from the crossbeam at the far end, exposing an eight-foot-long strip of yellowed snow and ice. As the stove warmed the air inside the shack, Sy moved methodically from board to board until he had opened a rectangle to the ice the size of a coffin. Then he took the ice pick from where he'd propped it outside the door and began chopping around the perimeter of the oblong opening.

"Talk to me," Sy said.

"No, Sy, you talk to me." In the light of day streaming through the double panes of plexiglass Sy saw the strange lumps in the coarse-woven jute, angles made by Wallace's elbows and knees. Blood seeped from the burlap across the boards of the floor and stained the snow in the hole. Wallace's head, arms, and a portion of sternum had been the first segment he'd discovered under the moon's albino glow. As a consequence, it rested at the bottom of the sack. The center bulged with Wallace's torso. Clipped at the thighs and chest, it had drained like a water main open at both ends when he'd picked it up. A hundred feet from the tracks in a clump of dead milkweed, Sy had found the legs; as if under such awesome weight, they'd snapped like matchsticks and been hurled straight, or almost straight, into the sky. Each was shod with a brown wingtip and a sock, but otherwise nude. They were so long, he'd had to fold them at the knees to fit them in the sack.

"I guess I don't need to tell you I'm a little upset," Sy said, jamming the blade of the pick into the ice below the floor. "I mean, it's like you, I should have expected it. You've always hurled yourself at the world without much regard for it, as if it were a trampoline or something." The blade of the pick punctured the ice, the loop of rope snagged his wrist. Green water gurgled up through the tiny one-inch hole and filled the rectangular gully he'd outlined. "Is that what you thought? That you'd bounce back."

"Sy, my daddy molded steel into train parts. I told you the story about being a kid and cutting my thumb on the wheel of a standing locomotive."

"That's about the only story you ever told me, Wallace."

"Let's just say, my family and I, we were like oil and water."

"You were the oil?"

"You could say that." Sy jammed the pick into the ice and threw his jacket and shirt onto the little fishing stool. The stove cooked the air inside the shack to a hundred and ten degrees because the valve couldn't be adjusted; it was either on or off, open or closed. In his undershirt Sy returned to his labor, sweat beading on his forehead and neck and stinging the corners of his eyes.

"To this day I don't know where you're really from. You show up, you've got nothing but a wired-together Mustang. I introduce you to some people, my Uncle Ned, my Uncle Ensign Wilder Powell, and suddenly, like water gushing through a busted beaver dam, the money's coming in, we're buying and selling, we're rich, you hear me, we're unbelievably, incredibly rich!"

"I told you. I'm from north of here."

"Canada?"

"North, Sy."

"The arctic then?"

"North of there even."

"Right, you're from the north pole, Wallace."

"I told you, but you've forgotten. The night I met you. I held your hand. I told you I'd grown lovesick and refused to dance."

"And that you came here, to northern Minnesota, to the iron range."

"I came for you, Sy."

"And splattered yourself over the whole north woods. You know something, collecting you this morning I had this crazy thought, that at the moment of impact, when the blood must've exploded out your legs and chest, little bits of you dropped from the sky into people's yards like shrapnel, like meteor dust, and became the waddling plastic ducks we sold, the artificial rocks, the birdbaths."

"In a sense, that is what happened."

"It was garish and awful and tasteless."

"Tasteless?"

"I can't believe I was so completely suckered." Now the fat slab of ice floated freely in the water beneath the floor of the shack. With the blade of the pick Sy pushed it under the water away from the hole and stationed it under the ice. Into the open rectangle he peered, into the shafts of refraction and the blackening depths.

"I love you, Sy Johnson."

Coated with sweat, Sy lifted the dripping gunnysack from the corner of the shack and held it over the opening with both arms as if it were a huge swinging pendulum. "Kawasachong. Lujinida. Wantonwah," he said. "Wisini. Kivandeba. Ashigan." The weight pulled in his shoulders, arms, and back, but he held the sack outward, so that it hung over the hole. "Gabimichigami. Kekekabic. Bingshick." He lifted it above his shoulders, so that the blood that had once united them might drain onto his neck and his chest in fluid strings, strings that might continue to unite them. The coarse jute cut his palms, the weight pulled in his lower back, hamstrings, and thighs, but the moment of submergence, of departure and loss, had to be borne fully or not at all. At last he was able to say it: "Good riddance, Wallace Triangle."

"A lie."

"What is?"

"Riddance."

He released the sack and it hit the water with a boulder-sized splash. It rested for a time amid the myriad floating chunks of ice, then sank straight and fast to the bottom of the lake—a ghost wizening into a mirror. Sy knelt on the floor of the shack. He peered into the water at his own eyes. The bottom was twenty feet below him, all rocks and crevices, which in the spring and summer snipped fishing line better than a razor. He saw nothing save his own reflection, no shade of beige, willowed and disjointed by the depths, nothing. With the pick, he pried the fat slab out from underneath the ice, and it buoyed back into place as snugly as a bar of soap into a soapdish. He scooped some slush and snow into the corner where Wallace had rested and scrubbed the blood from the boards with his hands. Then he washed his hands with some fresh slush and laid each of the removed boards neatly into place over the hole. When he had hammered each board back to the crossbeams, he grabbed the pick and went outside onto the ice.

The sun shone down blindingly now. In view of the plexiglass window, Sy chopped four fishing holes in a rectangle approximately four by eight feet. From each of the four Fish-N-Flags he unraveled three and a half arm lengths of line and secured two two-ounce sinkers six inches from each hook. To each of the four lines, he hooked a minnow, neatly, just below the spine. He let each line drop until the sinker pulled it taut to the spool, then he tested each of the four spring-loaded flags. He tugged a little at each line, and when the flag popped up, he pressed it down and set it over the hole. Then he reentered the shack, sat down on the little fishing stool, and watched the flags through the window.

It wasn't long before a flag popped up. Sy rushed onto the ice and, pinching the line between his thumb and finger, set the hook into the mouth of the fish. He felt a static resistance, like a loose board. He pulled the line up hand over fist until the fish came through the hole and lay there, breathing on the snow. It was a walleyed pike, big but not overly so, with pupils as white as the ice. It flipped itself several times with its tail, as if only then aware of the dimension of air into which it had ascended. He stationed it with his boot and tugged on the line until its gills showed in its mouth. Then he gave the line a quick yank and they dislodged onto the ice, useless as wax lips.

Inside the shack, he lay the fish on a cutting board on the counter next to the sink. While it still breathed, he placed the long thin blade of the fillet knife on its scales, as close to its pectoral fin as he could, then in a smooth sawing stroke, cut until he felt the firmness of its spine under the knife. He angled the knife then, trimming the meat from the fish's flank. When he came to the tail, he pressed the fillet back as if breaking in the binding of a book and took off the skin. He turned the fish over and did the same thing to its other side. Then he cut the two fillets, which were about eight inches long and three quarters of an inch thick, into as many bite-sized pieces as he had No. 2 barbed hooks, and into each of the soft white wedges he lodged one of the curled, sharp pieces of metal. He turned on a burner on the range, daubed a spoonful of lard into a pan, and set it over the circle of blue flame. When the lard was sizzling, he scooped up the pieces of fish and dumped them onto the pan to fry. The grease spattered and popped. He turned the pieces of fish over with a fork until they were cooked through and brown on both side. He salted and peppered them while they were still in the pan, then he forked them all onto his plate. "No riddance, eh, Wallace?" He sat back down on the little fishing stool and stared out the window with his plate of hot fish. One of the flags wafted in the cold, but he didn't care. He forked each morsel into his mouth and swallowed it, hook and all, without chewing. Then he washed the plate off in the sink, lay down on the floor of the shack, softly, as if in expectation of love, and began doing sit-ups. This was how he had determined to take himself out of the world.

SY PASSED AN HOUR SUFFERING QUIETLY. WITH EACH CON-traction, the barbs hooked deeper into the wall of his stomach. Clots formed, a hundred holes tried to heal, but with each contraction, he felt the blood stream into his stomach like liquid through a colander. When it was full, he would force the blood up his esophagus into his lungs and drown himself from the inside. Fingers locked behind his head, knees bent, eyes shut in an exercise of self-mastery, he had swallowed seeds of his own destruction, like Niswi, Wagosh, Eskwagama, con men of legend who swallowed seeds of the water hemlock, petals of the deadly nightshade, rhizomes of the blue flag iris, and saving their many faces, had become gods of the spring, summer, and fall. The seeds he had swallowed were those of the long-spined rose. With each contraction, he watered its roots. With each contraction, he felt its stalk thickening and pushing upward, its thorned limbs uncoiling and probing for breathable air and space to blossom.

He thought of spring, its tepid gusts warming the world above and below the division of ice. The frozen plate on which he and the tiny fishing shack rested would wizen into a sheet, a membrane, through which the cinder blocks would plummet. Then, perhaps a day or two later, the fishing shack itself would begin to fill up with water, through pores in the sheeting, through cracks in the floor and ceiling, through vents. A day or two after that, there'd be no sign at all of his undoing, save for an occasional bub-bling, a lure snagged from a passing canoe, a bit of flotsam. Through the planking tall weeds would rise, drawing spawn-bloated fish through the windows and door. As the roof fell, the stalks would force themselves through the tiny perforations, or make perforations where there were none, like sidewalk dande-lions, like trees rooted in rock. The tank of propane would settle into the mud, as all boulders eventually did, becoming a pocket of marsh gas sealed for eternity in sediment. His body was hardly worth considering. The muscles, tendons, ligaments, heart,spleen, lungs, cornea, penis, brain would be nibbled on by fish and turned into thin coils of excrement. In time, when his bones and teeth had decalcified and spread through the lake like spores of cottonweed borne on the wind, perhaps then, then, his two gold fillings would lie there for a time and shimmer back at the sun.

"Sy! You in there?" The voice belonged to his Auntie Barto. He recognized her shrill tremor. "I've come for my birdseed. I paid for it. It's mine by right." When her voice first came to him, he was halfway between sitting up and lying down, his abdomen like bread dough wrapped around a roller of nails. He lay back and felt the muscles stretch out and drain like wet sponges. "Heck's out here with me. You and Wallace make yourselves decent now. If you don't come to the door on the count of three, Heck here's gonna bust it down. You can't go breaking promises to people. Hello? One."

"I'm here, Barto," he said.

"I know it," she said. "Two."

He stood up, half expecting the door to burst open and the old man to fall headlong onto the floor before him, crumpled up in his army-issue trench coat, beady-eyed behind his inch-thick lenses with the heavy black frames. "Three."

He swallowed the paste thickening in the back of his throat. "I'm serious," said his aunt. "You boys put some clothes on. Lord knows I'm not one to shy away from a naked man, but Heck's here."

He opened the door and met his auntie's mufflered face, pink from the cold, a quarter inch of rouge, and her undeniable health. Beyond her, toeing the gills over the snow with his boot, stood Heck Miller in his glasses and coat. "Hey, Sy," he said, "looks like you caught one." He motioned at the popped up flag. "Looks like you got another on the line."

"I saw Wallace's car on the landing," said Barto. "I was worried about you two." Sy blocked her entrance with his chest. To her, his undershirt looked stained with fish blood, nothing more.

"Here." He handed her the keys to the Mustang. "Your order's in the trunk."

Barto sized him like an owl. "Is it sacked? I don't want it if it isn't sacked."

The question stunned him—her birdseed always came in sacks. She curled her neck around the jamb of the door. "Where's Wallace?" she asked. "I expected him to be here with you." As she nudged him out of the way, he coughed up a little flower of blood over her shoulder onto the snow. Heck examined him quizzically, then strode up to the entrance and to the propped-up ice pick. Sy unsheathed the fillet knife and held it within a whisker of the old man's throat.

"Stay outside," he said. "This is family." The old man's eyes receded and turned inward. Through the lenses they told nothing, like eclipsed planets. Sy jerked the thin tempered steel away from the old man's neck and sheathed it out of view of his aunt. Then he bolted the door from the inside.

"It's all right," said his aunt. "Heck likes the outdoors. Sometimes it's all you can do to get him to come inside and eat. It's nothing personal. He likes you. He told me so on the way up. He'd just rather fish than do anything else." She sat down on the little fishing stool, her auburn hair to the window. Her strong, wide knees made a perfect little table for a cup of tea and perhaps a brownie on a napkin. "Sy," she said, "how are you? How is Wallace?"

Her eyes pleaded with him as if for the latest gossip. Brown, firelit, her eyes would still be playful when she turned one hundred. "Wallace is all right, I guess. He laid down on the tracks last night and let a train run over him."

Sy watched the breath leave her, saw her eyes reach out from behind her strawberry-tinted lenses like strange, temperate suns. "He was sick, Auntie."

"How sick?"

"What he had a person doesn't live through." Sy saw her shock and sorrow turn to anger. "He gave it to me, Auntie." Lifting up his undershirt, Sy showed her the blemishes that seemed to float on the surface of his skin like curled red petals.

"Well, let's get you to a doctor. Heck sees someone in Isabella. Says he's awfully good. Says he's the only doctor who can make the—"

"Wallace went. The doctor only made him sicker." The doctor, in fact, had phoned to tell him that Wallace had left the hospital. When the night nurse had discovered Wallace's vacant bed, the IV needle removed from his arm and pressed into the mattress, the doctor had gotten right on the phone. More paste collected in the back of Sy's throat and he coughed a little of it into his hand. Barto watched him press the blood into his undershirt. The stain made a depot for the long, red tracks Wallace had made through the gunnysack. His auntie blushed but she did not turn away from nakedness or suffering. "It's only a matter of time," said Sy. The compassion he saw in her eyes now only embarrassed him, and he wished he had dropped off her birdseed before he ever went looking for Wallace. He could have wrapped the body parts in tar paper and looped it together with jumper cables.

"Can you walk, Sy?"

"Sure I can walk, walk twenty-five miles if need be." He hadn't realized it until then, but he was feeling better and better, as if he had lived his whole life in a state of hunger, a hunger that was only now, for the first time, being properly fed. His contentment differed from any Thanksgiving feast he'd ever experienced. It was as if his stomach were filled to the hilt with breast meat and rice pudding, corn chowder and mashed potatoes, but he felt light, as if a walk of fifty miles might wear him down as little as an after-dinner traipse through the woods to Barto's boat dock.

"You're coming with Heck and me back to the car, Sy."

"No, Auntie."

"Then there's nothing I can do. You and Dean. You were the spitting image of each other. There are remedies I know how to make, with water from this lake. Every autumn I dry out leaves of the mayapple, fruits of the skunk cabbage, petals of the marsh marigold. I could've helped Dean. I could've applied a paste to his temples. But he wouldn't let me because he'd given up the will to live. I could help you too, if you'd let me."

"There was nothing physically wrong with Dean," Sy said. He caught himself against the wall of the shack, where in 1979, married and with kids, Dean had scratched with the point of a knife, I AM HAPPY AND GAY, HAPPY AND GAY, HAPPY AND GAY. "Dean left the world because he was unfulfilled. That's the difference, Auntie. I'm leaving a world Dean could only dream of, a world that has made me very, very happy."

"Then I'll take the Mustang to the dump and just leave it there." He watched her strong hands unbolt the door. "If it's your wish to vanish without a sign, I'll simply tell people I don't remember you. They'll think it's Alzheimer's. And in time, I probably will."

"Will what?"

"Forget you."

As she opened the door, Sy saw the old man leaning against the ice pick. Heck waved at them. "You caught a dead body, Sy." The old man was trembling. "I'm telling you there's a body under the ice." Sy stepped onto the ice and saw the pale, blue arm. It extended from the fishing hole as if from a rolled-up sleeve. Heck had turned the palm to the snow and stationed it to the ice with a jack-knife. The dark cherry handle emerged from the knuckles like the grip of a rubber stamp. Sy knelt beside it as the old man chopped, his thick hair jerking like a raven at kill. "It's too wide. It won't fit through the hole." Heck had almost connected the four holes. A few chops more and the rectangular slab of ice would be floating on the surface of the lake. Sy pressed two of his fingers into the cold wet wound the knife had made. He saw, through the tip of the ring finger, the hook that had snagged it, and the loops of thin aqua-colored monofilament. A minnow, skewered to Wallace's blue, perfectly manicured nail, huffed for air. Sy tugged at the wrist, but Wallace's shoulder, some eighteen inches below the ice, kept it from coming up.

"I think we should leave it there," Barto said. "We've got no business exhuming the dead."

"Give me that," said Sy. He grabbed the ice pick from underneath Heck Miller's heaving neck.

"Heck, I think we should go."

"We can't go," said the old man. "There's a body down there. It's our responsibility to pull it up. It might be someone we know."

"I don't think it is," Barto said and looked longingly at the path of boot marks they had made in the snow. Sy drove the ice pick through the last few inches of the outline Heck had made on the frozen lake. His body no longer pained him. With each chop, more water gurgled up onto the slab. When the slab floated freely, he pushed it under the ice with the pick and saw the body of his lover lurking below the surface like a huge, fleshy fish. Then he moved the slab of ice under the body of Wallace Triangle and slowly, the slab of ice raised it into the cold air. He was nude, his limbs blue-veined and tendinous. In his hair, long weeds were entwined. For a time the three of them stared at the pockets of silt his mouth and eyes had become, as if in his face they expected to see the first signs of returned life. Then Sy removed his shirt and let it fall to the ice. He removed his boots and socks so that he stood barefoot in the snow. Then he unbuckled his belt and let his trousers and undershorts fall to his feet.

"Look at the son of a bitch!"

"We've got to let him, Heck."

Sy crawled onto the slab of ice and cleaved himself to the base of Wallace's trunk. As ice and water crested the slab, Wallace's face and shoulders went under, and Sy felt the sting, then the numbing, of water closing over his shoulders, back, and buttocks. "Kawasachong," said Barto. "Lujinida. Wantonwah."

Under water, Sy found Wallace's tongue and took it in his mouth, clammy and hard as a root. "Wisini. Kivandeba. Ashigan." He wrapped his arms around Wallace's head and kissed his lover as deeply as he could, then he rolled his lover's body on top of him, dislodging the pin in his hand, and through the closing waters saw, beyond the face of his own Auntie Barto, beyond the tin roof of the fishing shack, the exposed rock of Baskatong Hump, golden against the sky. "Gabimichigami. Kekekabic. Bingshick." Through the depths he and Wallace plummeted, sideling fish, sideling weeds, until one of the sharp-pointed rocks underneath the lake touched Sy's back and Wallace pressed it into his spine.

WHAT REMAINED OF THE DAY HECK MILLER SPENT PULLING up fish through the tiny fishing holes. Each one he unhooked he gave to Barto to clean inside the shack. As the afternoon passed, the slab of ice on which the two boys had rested froze again into place, so that there was hardly a seam left of the rectangle that had been. Barto would have the fish cleaned by now, he thought, as he reeled the lines into the spools of the Fish-N-Flags. He snapped the flags into place and set them on the red plastic sled. He didn't have many years left, he knew, but in those that remained, he would put the equipment to good use.

Inside the shack, Barto handed him his plate of hot fish. As the world outside the window darkened, he and Barto ate in silence. Later, when they had finished and were sipping their coffee by the light of one candle, she said, "Heck, I remember when Sy's mother used to bring him to the cottage. The men would be out fishing. I'd strip him down to his bare skin and stand him on the picnic table out back. I'd fill up a bucket of water from the pump.

It had a huge, red handle. Then I'd scrub him down until his body smelled as sweet as the balsams."

"I had a nephew," said Heck then. "But he went to Rupholding, Germany, of all things—to raise sheep. I haven't heard from him since. It's a shame, I can't even remember his name."

"Heck, did I ever tell you my mother was Swedish. My father, he was full-blood Indian, but my mother, she used to talk on and on of the fjords."

"No, Barto, you never told me that." Heck watched the eyes he loved glisten and turn inward, and then his own vision, which had never been very good, also turned inward, and he remembered all the gigantic fish he had ever pulled up through the ice.

Perhaps an hour passed. Barto looked at him and said, "Come lie with me on the floor, Heck."

He crouched to the floor despite the pain in his brittle joints. He put his old, dry lips to her ear, his hand on her breast. In this manner, he drifted to sleep. Sometime close to three, as was his way, he woke up. He picked himself up off the planks, lit the range, and set a pan of water to boil. Then he stepped outside onto the frozen lake. The sky was starry and clear. To the north, beyond the silhouette of pine tops, lights of many colors leapt and spiraled. "Barto!" he called. "Come and see!"

His love stepped through the open door, and he put his arm around her. "It's a rare sight. You don't normally see them this time of year."

"What?" she asked as if still in dream.

"The northern lights." He looked at her and he saw her see them.

"You know what I read?"

"What, Barto?"

"That the northern lights have been around as long as the Earth itself, but what makes those beautiful colors—"

He felt her wrap her arm around his side. "Pollution, Heck. It's the sun shining through a bunch of toxic fumes, car exhaust, and chemical debris."

"They sure are something."

"Yes," she said, "they surely are." Then, as two lonely old figures, they watched the garish pinks, yellows, and blues dance like savages above the world.

BIRDS

A POET, AMANDA HAD DONE THINGS SHE HADN'T WANTED
to. She hadn't wanted to bartend or waitress, but those were staple
employments, she figured, for anyone with lofty aims. Nor had she
wanted to strip, but whenever the grit and grime of food and
beverage service crept into the private, soulful space of her being,
she rode a cab down Second Street into Albuquerque's industrial
sector, strode up the awning-covered steps into D.J.'s Showclub,
and asked Dolores Jane for a spot in the evening's lineup.

Dolores Jane, whose initials appeared in pink cursive on
the neon sign outside, balked each time she asked. "You can't be
coming back here forever, darling." There in a paneled office
where every girl who had ever danced at D.J.'s had a file, behind a
metal desk dappled with peels of mahogany contact paper, to the
side of a four-by-twelve-foot tempered pane that looked onto the
stages and seating, she sat, squat, pudgy, partial to heavy silver
jewelry from the pueblos and tropically colored moo-moos that
draped, the more empathic girls insisted, over a heart too big for its
own good.

"Still, it's good to see you, Mandy," she'd say, "what with those beefy breasts of yours and slender frame. Why I'd be a fool to send you across town to Max, or Reginald, or, God forbid, Deiter." Her face freckled from her receding hairline to her triple chin, she'd cup her puffy cheeks in her fat palms, so that her orange hair stuck out like shoots of a cactus that had outgrown its pot. Then a flick of wrists that amazed Amanda, for it occurred without a crash of pottery, and the creased face—with its pasted-on lips and brothy eyes that looked as if they'd sooner spill from their sockets than endure another hard-luck tale from one of her girls—remained, suspended in an admixture of tobacco smoke, liquor, and gaudy perfume. "No, you'll dance for me, sweetheart, and it'll be just like old times."

"God, I hope not," Amanda would answer, taking in the dented file cabinets, the yard-sale vases burgeoning with convenience-store roses, and the six crookedly hung portraits of Dolores Jane's six Siamese tomcats, each bearing a man's name—"Ferdinand," "Instacio," "William"—on a brass plate fastened to the frame, as if they were features of a bus depot she went to on the holidays, familiar things seen in transit to a place—or state—even more familiar.

"Now why's that? Haven't you ever been happy here?"

"I've quit," Amanda would say, "only once less than I've returned."

"True. I'm afraid you're one of those who wish the world other than it is."

"That's me."

"Maybe this time it will be, pudding. It's all in how you look at it—whether you're able to view things from the proper perspective."

A thoughtful nod. "I suppose distance is everything."

This time, though, Amanda was returning under grimmer circumstances. She'd had a colonoscopy, and a digestive disorder that had plagued her since childhood with watery diarrhea and burning discharges of putrid gas had been diagnosed as ulcerative colitis. Because she hadn't reported her symptoms until recently, a riddled portion of her lower intestine would have to be removed. The pathologist who'd examined her, a female doctor sympathetic to her mired financial situation, was willing to postpone her recommendation for surgery until after Amanda regained employment with health benefits, and for this Amanda was grateful. At the restaurants where she worked, managers scoffed at requests for coverage, while Dolores Jane provided it to everyone, from dancers to bouncers, as a matter of course.

On the afternoon of Amanda's return, Dolores Jane forewent the usual pleasantries. "It seems your sabbaticals are getting shorter and shorter, sweetness. How long was this last one? Four, five weeks?"

"Don't worry," Amanda replied in a voice so resigned it surprised her, "this time I'm here to stay."

Her doctor had explained to her that the operation would not cure her colitis, only remove the affected tissue—though by maintaining a modified low-fiber diet and implementing a regimen of vitamin supplements and cortisone suppositories, she might reduce, though never eliminate, her need for further surgery. Barium enemas coupled with regular colonoscopies and sigmoidoscopies, as a safeguard against the disease's spreading, would make periodic hospital visits necessary. In worst case scenarios, which Amanda didn't want to consider, patients went through life having sections of their digestive tracts cut out. When their bowels became too foreshortened to process waste, colostomies were performed, holes made in their abdominal walls, to which bags were attached to collect materials they could no longer pass. All of this her doctor had articulated with startling frankness.

"Nonsense," Dolores Jane replied. "Only I am here to stay." The doughy folds of her jowls wagged as her olive-black pupils slunk toward the window. On the other side of it, an emaciated peroxide blonde Amanda knew only by her stage name, Starr, performed an uninspired twirl around the pole. "Take Starr, honey. The girl's twenty-seven going on sixty-seven. Now if she'd gone to college when she was making money, acquired an education instead of a heroin habit and two sadly defective children, hers might've been a different story. She might've experienced a blossoming, a period of exponential growth, a moment at the height of her radiance when she took stock of, and in, her future. Such things happen, and not as infrequently as a person might think. But they didn't for her, the poor thing, and now I don't know what I'm going to do with her. Replace her with a potted palm?"

"Aren't you asking a little much of Starr?" Amanda queried.

"Of course I am, sugar. I ask it of all my girls, to know when their time's up. But it's like expecting fine wines to tell me when they're to be drunk." She daubed moisture from her cheeks with a tissue. "But you're smarter than that, and I know in my heart of hearts you'll step down when the time comes."

"So I'm back on?"

"Of course, child," said Dolores Jane. "You haven't gained a pound in all the years I've known you, and your face is simply one of the prettiest ever to grace my establishment."

Relieved, Amanda curled her lower lip and blew air up into her bangs. "Then on with the paperwork."

"Oh, paperwork schmaperwork," said Dolores Jane. "Truth is,

honey, you have a way of coming back before I can get around to undoing your paperwork. Of course, I'm no longer the powerhouse I was once." Dolores Jane gawked at her supinely, her face so wrinkled it was hard for Amanda to imagine its ever being young.

"So I have health?"

"And, I believe, life."

"Life?"

"I believe you have life insurance, girl." Dolores Jane chuckled kindly, and Amanda felt her mood improve as crests of blubber churned like laundry beneath her boss's lemon-lime batik. "Goodness me, remember when you first started dancing, I asked you to name a beneficiary?"

"Vaguely, yes," said Amanda. She'd been twenty-four at the time, and she was thirty-four now. "Can you tell me who I listed?"

"If you'll give me a second." Dolores Jane swiveled on her chair, then thumbed through a battered drawer of dog-eared files until she located Amanda's. "Ah, here we are. You named Larissa. You wish to keep her or name someone new?"

Now it was Amanda's turn to sigh. "I'll keep her. I just can't believe Larry and I have been together ten years." It seemed impossible.

IN AN ENTRYWAY DWARFED BY CORINTHIAN ARCHES OF red velvet wallpaper Amanda said hello to Ricky and Marvin, bouncers whose white gloves, black tails, pleated dress shirts, and combined weight of over five hundred pounds put a razor's edge on the security they provided. Gay black men, they removed nuisances, without stress or strife, often before one knew he was one. "Yo! Mandy!" said Marvin, holding out a fleshy slab of palm, which she dutifully slapped. "Thought you'd said sayanara to all of us stuck in Boobyland."

"Guess again," Amanda replied lightheartedly as Ricky grazed her shawl-covered shoulder with his finger, then backed away shaking his hand as if to cool it.

"You still hot. I swear you ain't come down even one degree."

"To stay that good looking," said Marvin, "you must've been eating right, working out every day. Aren't I right?"

Amanda shook her head, not about to tell them about her colitis or how it kept her from gaining weight. "Just living," she replied.

"Well, Marvin and I have a proposition for you. Don't say no until you've heard us out. See, we went in together on a health club, and not your usual, run of the mill health club either. Sure, it's equipped with everything the others have—climbers, rowers, weight machines, free weights—but we've also got what the others don't, namely a private training room for exotic dancers. In such a place you can work on your body without being stared at and potentially recognized by the losers who frequent crappy joints like this."

"You see, we've eliminated the 'dis' from discomfort," said Marvin. "Hey Ricky, give Mandy a coupon."

"Free, two-week trial membership," Amanda read. "Thanks." She folded the new pink punchcard in half between the five fives and six books of matches with which she'd stocked a gold-clasped patent leather purse. "I'll think about it."

"You do that," said Ricky.

As she passed the bar she smiled at Katie, in the middle of making a gimlet, and Katie fluttered her fingers in a wave, breasts jiggling in the riveted vee of a biker's leather corset. It felt good to be back, returning to a set of expectations that enabled her to revert to the person everyone expected her to be, though the seating area was rather sparsely occupied, she decided, blue collars sadly outnumbering white by a ratio of three or four to one. Still, under black lights, which ran in glowing lilac tubes along the support pillars and crossbeams, seven or eight white collars stood out in the haze like dangled envelopes, stiff, promising.

At the deejay's booth, she handed her selections to Bobby. How Bobby had lost his legs was anyone's guess, but he'd spun disks for Dolores Jane for years, hand-propelling himself up a ramp a few minutes before the club opened and hand-propelling himself back down a few minutes after it closed. He subsisted on green chili cheeseburgers and curly fries, prepared in the kitchen and delivered, at his insistence, by a dancer with her top off. Most girls reluctantly obliged, costing them five minutes at most and seeming the least they could do for one who might, given half a reason, get their songs wrong or keep them on stage longer than their allotted ten and a half minutes.

As Bobby looked over her sheet, heavily tinted aviator glasses slid down the bridge of his beak-like nose. "Need anything special, Mandy? Laser effects? Fog?" His voice, nasally and girlishly alto when he spoke in person, was nonetheless as modulated and detached as a late night radio announcer's when it came over the sound system.

"Some fog," said Amanda, "on the second track."

"'Three Times a Lady' by the Commodores. It's as good as done." From an array of pens and mechanical pencils clipped to a pocket protector, Bobby withdrew a Mont Blanc and made a notation next to her choices. "I'm sure glad you're back, Mandy. I missed you."

"I missed you too, Bobby," she said.

"Say, any chance of your bringing me my supper tonight?"

"Still eating at ten?"

Bobby nodded.

"You've got it."

In the changing room she found Starr, feet clumped in the twisted shanks of her cowboy boots. Amanda opened a locker beside hers as she threw her arms in frustration. "Mind helping me with these, hon?" Starr asked. "I swear these new dogs're tight as traps."

Without thinking, Amanda stepped over the wooden bench on which the woman forlornly sat and took hold of a crimson boot. Starr bit her lower lip and pushed, blood rushing to her otherwise sallow complexion, yet the Tony Lamas just hung there, limp as a bucket of restaurant ketchup. "Push harder," Amanda coached.

Starr closed her eyes and did, and Amanda decided that her face was actually two, one transposed upon the other like images on film that jittered in and out of alignment. One was young and pretty, the other ragged, ancient.

When her heel had inched into the boot's heel, Starr said, "If we can get one, we can get the other. I'm sure of it," smiling weakly as Amanda picked up the second boot.

She was alone with the woman, the incessant bump and grind pulsating through the bulb-studded vanity mirrors of seven make-up stations, each with its community hair sprays and nipple enhancement aerosols, its lipsticks, mascaras, and eyeliners. Yet in minutes the balance of the evening shift would be arriving, cackling about one thing or another, and Amanda had hoped for some time by herself in one of the toilet stalls before they did.

"There," said Starr. "I think we got 'em." Beaming, she stood up from the bench and took a few wobbly steps on the cement floor. "That was awfully kind of you. Just thought you'd like to know."

"Hunh?" said Amanda.

"I thought you'd like to know how awfully kind that was of you. Some people can't tell the difference, and when they aren't told, they can't help straying from the glorious path God set for them."

Amanda unzipped her athletic bag and began arranging her outfits on hangers—the black leather bondage bra and T-bar bottom, the heather-gray one-piece boxer pajamas with ecru lace hem, the short tie-sarong and bikini top in a floral sea pattern—all, thankfully, tax write-offs.

"If you promise not to take it personal," Starr continued, "I'll tell you your kindness sort of took me by surprise," twining hair bleached to the white of a fried egg around her index finger.

"Oh?" said Amanda. "How's that?"

"Now you're Mandy, right?" Amanda nodded. "You're the one who leaves and comes back, leaves and comes back? Well, I gather some of the other dancers have had a hard time with that. You seem sweet as a blueberry to me, but I've heard a few of the girls complaining. Stuck up, I believe, were the words they used to describe you. But I disagree with them."

She supposed the other dancers had been venting hostility about her work ethic, their words spoken out of professional jealousy; still, it hurt to hear what they'd said about her. "Know thyself," said Amanda. "That's what Socrates counseled."

"I'll have to ponder that one," Starr said with a laugh that sounded like a hiccup. "Geez Louise, I was supposed to pick up my little 'uns from special daycare ten minutes ago. You probably heard they're not quite right mentally."

"I'm sorry," Amanda said. "I did hear."

"Well, it's people's perogative to talk, so talk they will. But there's nothing to be sorry about as far as my children are concerned. Oh, I don't doubt my lifestyle messed with them some, but they're the sweetest darned things. Honestly, I wouldn't trade 'em for a sales lot of Malibus."

She flashed Amanda a fleeting, gum-popping smile. "Listen, gotta run, but I want you to know it's been a treat getting to know the real Mandy."

Not until a blast of drums and bass muffled the clumpety-clump of Starr's boots and the door closed shut behind them did the irony of the woman's parting words register in dimensions as multifold as the petals of a dark and cancerous rose. By then Amanda stood in a locked stall, peering down at a syringe afloat in the toilet bowl. Remembering what Dolores Jane had said about Starr, how the girl might have made something of herself, Amanda worked the flush lever and watched the calibrated tube flex between gush and trap, then buoy back to the surface when the water calmed. Amanda pulled down her leggings, sat down on the still-warm seat, and felt the pressure in her abdomen dissipate as her bowels unharbored contents as liquidy as they were noxious. Amanda flushed again before the fumes could rise, then lit an entire book of matches to mask the odor. The real Mandy? Who, or what, that was could make her gag.

BY THE TIME AMANDA RETURNED TO THE SEATING AREA IN her sarong and bikini top, the changing room had filled with dancers plucking hairs and camouflaging blackheads, hooking bra straps and fastening g-strings, and the crowd had doubled. In stiletto heels that matched her purse, she spotted a white collar she recognized as a regular, strode confidently across the club to him, and asked him if he wanted a table dance. An older gentleman with a trimmed mustache and kind eyes, he raised his zephyr weight sleeves as if powerless against her charms. Amanda set her purse beside his scotch highball and, as "U Can't Touch This" by M. C. Hammer blended with "I'll Be Good to You" by the Brothers Johnson, unhooked her cups so that her breasts fell to eye level.

The dupe was neatly groomed and nicely appareled, his business suit pressed and velvety-looking under the black lights, his tie a tasteful paisley print. When Amanda sandwiched his face between her tits, his shaved cheeks felt as smooth as chamois, and curling over the fragile crown of his head, she whispered into his ear that she liked his cologne. When she ran her crotch along the pleat in his slacks, the material felt rich between her thighs. Planting her rear on the rise in his lap, she arched her back so he could look over her shoulder at the cleft of her massive, pendulous, and completely natural double Ds. As he did, she stroked his scrotum through the fabric and, with her free hand, heaved one breast and then the other to her lips and sucked on the nipples. She supposed she was lucky. Saucer-sized and tawny in hue, her aureoles needed no sprays or ointments to keep them engorged and pert.

For ten songs she danced only for him, using her sarong as a see-through curtain. Fresh scotches arrived at his table, money changed hands, and as he entered a perfumed netherworld of swaying flesh glimpsed through sun-streaked hair, through palm fronds, acacia blossoms, and sea, her sense of purpose returned. Behind the bar, Katie rang a brass bell each time a customer tipped her for a cocktail. On both stages, women pranced, squatted, and did the splits, performed backbends, pirouettes, and arabesques; when green appeared stageside, a dancer crawled to it on all fours, spread her thighs, giving the beholder an exclusive view of pudendum triangulated by faux silk. Between sets, Bobby encouraged patrons to splurge on a fifty dollar trip to the V.I.P. Lounge and announced a limited, three-song special on pitchers of Bud, his rhapsodizing so disk-jockey that Amanda was always a little thrown by how homely he was in person. Around her, dancers not on stage gave table dances, their slender frames illuminated crescents, and she was one of them, a sliver of moon in a sky with twenty, as integral to the overall effect as a Titan, Calypso, or Iapetus.

When her name came over the loudspeakers—"PUT THOSE MEATHOOKS TOGETHER, FELLAS, FOR THE LOVELY, TALENTED, SOPHISTICATED MANDY!"—Amanda was ready for the main stage. Most girls preferred to work the floor, not only because they thought the money better, but because they preferred taking off their clothes before a pair of eyes than before fifty or a hundred fifty pairs. "THAT'S RIGHT! PUT 'EM TOGETHER!" But Amanda had never noticed any difference in the money other than that it came in the form of George Washingtons and Abraham Lincolns rather than Andrew Jacksons and Ulysses S. Grants, dead presidents whose victories had been at the expense of grunts and foot soldiers. "TELL ME YOU'VE EVER HAD BEAUTY LIKE THIS IN YOUR FACE, AND I'LL TELL YOU STRAIGHT-OUT YOU'RE A LIAR!" As for the number of eyes, what difference did it make if a thousand looked at you? A million couldn't possess you. And that, in a nutshell, was the beauty of it.

As the opening drum beat of "I'll Take You There" by the Staple Singers reverberated in her marrow, Amanda stepped into the lights in boxer pajamas as sheer as they were flattering. The stage was penis-shaped, and as she strutted down the shaft, seats encircling the testes filled with dupes whistling and clapping over the plucked bass line, then over Roebuck Staples' growl, "Ah-h-h know a place." Amanda leapt for the pole, spun like a barber's stripe six times before she reached the bottom. By then, the scrotum sac was furry with currency. She crawled to a one, her breasts heavy as cantaloupes against the stretched cotton, her nipples nubbins of heather gray, and presented a college-age dupe in a Harvard jersey an ecru laced valentine of her lithe and quivering cleavage. He grinned awkwardly, punching his buddy and pointing at a vision preserved now only in the vaults of his memory, for by then she was slithering along the arc of seated dupes, behind which dupes of every age, size, and status stood as solemnly as a choir of tenors. Not a single table dance was being had, and all the other dancers but one flocked together in a petroleum-slick, particolored cloud beneath the neon Silver Bullet sign, time marked by a teetering calf, a preening of hair, a breath of smoke. On the small stage, the girl known as Pint Size danced topless for herself alone.

If asked twelve years ago whether she'd ever resort to stripping, Amanda would've answered adamantly, "Never," and so it always made her a little wary of herself how naturally she manipulated the mechanics of magnetism, with what ease she assumed the roles of puppet and puppeteer both, at once pulling the strings and feeling their tug, at once creating an effect and being it. Dancing on stage was as simple as hedging a walk, only the weeds were transferable as legal tender, and as soon as she'd severed one, another sprouted in its place. When she'd fed a dupe his glimpse, she dusted the payment between her legs into a pile around the pole. There was no point in looking at the denominations—small as they were any acknowledgment only broke the spell—but as she rounded the second curve, she couldn't help noticing a hundred dollar bill at rest on the track like an odd tie. When this sort of thing happened, usually with a five or couple of ones, Amanda treated the dupe no differently than the others, for what act could she perform, short of merging with him in his seat, that wouldn't fail to give him his money's worth?

Amanda crawled to it and paused, in a breath fulfilling the tit-end of the contract, but before she could supply the ass-end, the music faded and lights dimmed. When they came back on, shining through blue gels, she was ensconced in fog pumped out through four ducts over which she stood with breasts exposed, tangled locks swept back, and knees angled in a likeness of Botticelli's *Venus*. The crowd applauded as the mist cleared and the wispy piano melody with which the Commodores began "Three Times a Lady" gave way to full symphonic orchestration. Behind her, the hundred dollar note lay where she'd tossed it, perched on the heap of ones like a butterfly testing its wings.

To the classic of bedroom soul, Amanda peeled her pajamas to her ankles and stepped from them. In her g-string and heels, she tended fires lit during her first song, beckoning with come-hither eyes each dupe to cross from darkness into light. Framing each winsome face between her undulating thighs, then dragging its paltry offering over the labial crease in a smidgen of silly dacron she was required, by law, to wear, she thought she understood what Einstein meant when he wrote about relativity, what Wittgenstein meant when he asked whether his hand was, in fact, a "hand." She was Echo, each dupe Narcissus, and though a cough could make her wet, she felt secure behind a scrim as transparent as it was impenetrable.

Amanda treated the second hundred dollar note no differently than she had the first, but by the time a third appeared, she'd so studied the dupe's face she could've identified it in a mugshot. He was, she supposed, a man men thought women found attractive— cleft chin, razored sideburns, narrow, sloping jaws. Her set over, she climbed down off the stage and asked him if he wanted to treat himself to a trip to the V.I.P. Lounge. "That way we can be alone," she explained.

"You're the most exquisite woman I've ever seen," he replied, his voice low, gravelly.

"Is that a yes or a no?" she asked.

"A yes," he answered, and she told him the terms, fifty dollars for a half hour, a hundred for a full, no touching, house rules. "Here's three hundred," he said. "And I'll sit on my hands."

"Three hours is a lot of dances. You're sure you can afford them?"

"You mean, I pay for each of those, too?" he inquired, and Amanda nodded. "Then I'll buy an hour, and you can keep the extra two hundred as a tip."

Amanda pursed the agreed upon amount and gave the rest to Katie, who rang it up on the cash register's Special Services key. "You're doing pretty well for yourself, aren't you tonight, lover girl?"

Amanda laughed. Katie, too, was a lesbian. "For myself?" she asked.

"I know. You've got Larissa's boys to support. How old are they now?"

"Fourteen and twelve."

"Well, kids are expensive, aren't they?" said Katie, who had none.

"You have no idea," said Amanda.

AMANDA RETURNED TO THE DUPE AND TOOK HOLD OF HIS hand. He wasn't the sort she would have gravitated toward on any night save a slow one. His hair unruly, his face gruffer than it should have been at his age, he had the look of one who had been to college but who'd done poorly for himself in the ten or twelve years afterward. To have flaunted so much money, he probably lived off a trust fund, his callouses the result of bumping between jobs he took for kicks.

She opened the V.I.P. Lounge with a key card and led him inside. "Relax," she said and pointed to one of six leather recliners with which the room was furnished, each angled away from the others and accompanied by a heavy endtable and reading lamp. The idea was to create the ambiance of a living room and, in so doing, cater to the customer's fantasy of bringing a dancer home. Amanda closed the door, into which a timer had been set, and the clamor to which she'd grown accustomed was snuffed as instantly as a pinched wick. They were alone. On one wall hung the mounted head of an antelope, on another, a framed, signed print of a Vargas girl. Beside a glass and brass entertainment system which included a wide-screen TV and stereo, a plaster-of-Paris chimney rose from the dome of a ceramic fireplace. Amanda flicked a switch on the wall to ignite it. As she slid a CD into the player, she asked him what he wanted to drink.

"A cognac would be fitting," he replied, "but I think I'll stick with Heineken."

From a cooler below the bar Amanda removed a bottle and a chilled glass. On a ledger she made a mark under the heading "Beer, Import." As the soft, sexy rhythms of Teddy Pendergrass descended from speakers hung from the four corners, she carried his order across the white shag. The sound wasn't truly quadraphonic, for a tweeter had been removed from one of the speakers, a hole cut in the grille, and a video camera installed for security purposes. "So what do you do?" she asked as she straddled him.

"I'm an artist," he answered. "I paint." She pressed a button which lowered the backrest electronically, opened his collar so that a few chest hairs curled out from his denim shirt. His khakis had shifted under her weight, and his erection rubbed against her through the slash pocket. A curler, she thought, grazing his cheeks with her breasts as she dimmed the lamp.

"You must be very successful."

He swallowed some beer. "Know what? I've been painting fifteen years, and I only sold my first this afternoon. Now I don't know if I'd call that successful or not."

"Everyone's got to start somewhere," Amanda encouraged. Some dupes took to the V.I.P. Lounge, others bottomed out in it. Amanda hoped he was one of the former.

"Jesus, one of those enameled, Santa Fe-style hausfraus from the Heights hears about me. How, I have no idea. But in she comes, Mrs. Sandals-and-Flouncy Skirt, through the rear entrance of the motorcycle accessory shop where I work no less, takes one look at the painting and wants it in her foyer." He paused. "Mind telling me what in God's name a foyer is."

"An entranceway." Amanda hoped it would surprise him that she knew.

"Well, she must've wanted it in there pretty badly. She paid me twelve hundred dollars on the spot for it."

"What's it of?" Amanda asked, "The painting?" for it didn't take an accountant to figure out he'd already spent half of what it had fetched on her.

"What's it of? It's of the conflict between being and non-being, figurative drawing and abstract, straight line and arced, two dimensionality and three. Need I go on?"

"Sounds like a lot of conflict for one picture," Amanda remarked half-jokingly, for she knew how difficult it was to talk about a poem. Better just to read it.

"Then I'll put it differently. It's of a naked woman. Only I thought her the most exquisite naked woman I'd ever seen until I came here and saw you."

Amanda considered this and said, "You understand, don't you, that I won't be totally nude for you."

"I understand," he said.

Amanda ground her flanks into the hard lump in his lap and pulled down her top so that her breasts hung between them like buffers from a pier. She gave him the standard fare, touches meant to whet the appetite but not to satisfy it. When his glass was empty, she brought him another beer. When his cigarette was out, she took another from his pack and lit it for him. With no more than five minutes left in their hour together, he removed his billfold and set its cash contents, $582, on the endtable.

"I want you to put a little more of yourself into it," he said. "I want you to give me the act you reserve for special customers."

He was less a dupe than a fool, she thought, for she'd already given him the act reserved for special customers and she could not put more of herself into it than she had already. "You want another hour?" she asked.

"I want the most my money can buy in the time I have left." Amanda tucked the money into her purse and went on as she had before, spiking her heels into the upholstery and alternating frontal views with views of her rear. It was turning into a good night moneywise; now if she could just keep her end-of-the-night depressions at bay. Dark and debilitating, they were what had kept her running back to food and beverage service. But with no more than a minute remaining, his fingers suddenly locked across her midriff, then a phlegmy swallowing as he thrust her, hips first, onto a knob in his slacks harder than any manhood.

"Maybe you didn't hear me," he whispered into her hair. "I want the most my money can buy."

Amanda didn't think she was hurt, and she knew better than to struggle, that hand contact was sufficient to set security measures into motion, but as he panted, his grip tightened and, in a hush between songs, forced gas from her loins try as she might to keep it from escaping. Not a lot squeaked out, but what did was potent, and as his hands released their hold, Amanda crawled from the recliner onto the carpet.

Wanting only to strike a match and relieve them both of the odor, she reached for her purse as Ricky and Marvin burst in through the door. They made a move for the dupe, then stepped back. "Good God," said Ricky as Marvin hankied his nose and mouth. "I believe this sorry excuse for a man has fouled his drawers." She thought he was going to laugh, then realized he was deadly earnest.

"What've you been eating, pal?" asked Marvin. "Smells ike chicken fingers been your staple for the past thirty-five years."

The artist stared at her with eyes world-weary and glazed as Ricky and Marvin heaved him by the shoulders from the chair. He made no attempt to correct the error, though had he no one would have believed him.

"Don't hurt him," Amanda said as they carried him out. The smell was so vile, so miasmic and rank she would've liked to believe it had come from anywhere but her.

When she'd put herself back together, Amanda worked her way toward the kitchen, dancing for fives and tens, and Bobby's burger and fries were waiting for her under heat lamps when she got there. She pulled down her top and took them to him, serving from the right as she'd been trained, though from the left would have been easier, his wheelchair squeezed in among equalizers and soundboards.

Without looking up from his dials and needles, Bobby thanked her, and as she came down from the booth, Katie waved to her from the bar. "You won't believe it, Mandy honey," she said before Amanda could take a seat, "but that dupe you were dancing for just shot himself in the head."

"You're kidding."

"Do I look like I'm kidding? Ricky and Marvin are outside talking to the cops." Katie spoke excitedly whenever anything bad happened to a dupe, her attitude toward the straight, white, patriarchal power structure that of a guerrilla. "So they throw him out, right? And he wanders around the parking lot a while. When Ricky and Marvin tell him they're phoning the police if he doesn't scram, he says, 'Don't bother. I'll call them myself.' Then he takes a gun out of his pants pocket—guess he had it with him the whole night—puts the barrel to his nose, and ka-chang, he's fucking gone, blood splattering six different patrons' cars. Can you imagine?"

"Jesus," said Amanda. "He put the gun to his nose?"

Katie nodded, wiping her hands on a wet bar rag. "Chock up another one to the Gipper."

ONCE SHE HAD CHANGED INTO HER BONDAGE BRA AND T-BAR bottom, Amanda told the cops she had no idea why Andrew Steven Lloyd had committed suicide, though she told them what she knew, that he'd spent approximately twelve hundred dollars in a little over an hour and that she'd felt the gun in his pocket, although she hadn't known it was such at the time. "What did you think it was?" the officer conducting the investigation asked her, but before she could reply his eyes fell on the taut laces of her bra, and he said, "Nevermind. I'm not stupid."

When Larissa dropped in a little after midnight, Amanda said nothing about passing gas on the lap of a customer. Her bowels had been a private matter for so long that to talk about them with any-one save her doctor amounted to breaching a sacred compact. "God, I feel shitty," she said when she was through.

"About what happened?" Larissa asked. "Or in general?"

"About what happened," Amanda said, though her depression felt a lot like the depressions that wrenched her every night at D.J.'s an hour or two before close, only worse because she felt nothing for Andrew Steven Lloyd. He'd been a dupe, she reproached her-self, but he'd also been a human being.

"Anything come in the mail?" Amanda asked, and Larissa smiled hopefully as she removed an envelope from her satchel, then slid it across the booth they were sharing in a far corner of the club. Addressed to her in her own hand, it undoubtedly contained a rejection from one of a dozen literary journals to which she'd sent poems. Though she'd told Larissa not to bring the SASEs on her visits, some of Larissa's optimism always rubbed off on her as she slid a sharp, red nail under the lip. The journals operated on shoe-strings; perhaps this one—from Lexington, Kentucky, she saw by the postmark—had sent its acceptance in her envelope to defray costs. Having never had a poem published, Amanda didn't know whether to expect a phone call or a letter from the editor who first decided her words worthy of print.

Amanda removed the note and silently read the printed mes-sage: "Sorry. Not for us."

"What's it say?" Larissa asked, and Amanda handed it back. To have a poem published, to have her words read by people who had never seen her and didn't know her, would wrap all the disparate elements of her life into a package and unite them in meaning, meaning others could grasp and possibly cherish and, in connect-ing her to a world to which she felt no connection, make whatever she did for a living worth it. Until then, she'd simply have to deal with each depression as it struck.

"Larry," she said, "you mind waiting till close? It's only an hour and a half away, and it would save my having to take a cab."

"Oh, Mandy." The tendons of Larissa's neck flexed at the men-tion. Amanda hated even to ask—she knew how important it was for one of them to be up in the morning with the boys, to fix them breakfast and see them out the door to the busstop. And it wasn't as if Larissa lazed around the house all day; she managed a bird shop, and at night she had to feed the young, the baby macaws and African grays, the fledgling parakeets, cockateels, and budgies, some of which sold for a $1000 a pop. But the depression she was experiencing felt as bad as any.

"Forget it. I'll be home in a couple hours." She got up from the table, her short fuse weighting her even more. Of course, writing poems brought her joy, even if no one but Larissa read them, and as she danced, the movements of her body brought happier thoughts to bear. Her relationships with the boys were good—as far as they knew, she was a bartender and waitress—and they treated her like a second mom. And she loved Larissa, crazy as a loon though she could be, filling the house with birds she refused on principle to cage. But when Bobby announced that D.J.'s was closed and house lights lit up the crushed butts, spilled cocktails, and tawdry wallpaper, her thoughts turned again to birds. She disliked them, her home was overrun with them, and at close it could seem as if all her efforts went to seed, literally and figuratively.

Wrapped again in her shawl, Amanda tipped out at the bar and discovered the gift certificate to Ricky and Marvin's health club. If the surgery was successful, she'd put on weight, possibly a lot, according to her doctor. To keep dancing she'd have to add exercise to the regimen; what with meeting the boys when they came home after school and cleaning up after the birds—it seemed as if every other month there was another—she'd have no time to write, and what was the point of dancing if she couldn't write? The point, she decided, was that it enabled her to do her part in supporting the family; still, the boys would do perfectly well without a second mother if their first could be freed, and as she stepped gingerly over police tape into night air that tingled against her skin, she thought she knew a way.

Second Street was a busy thoroughfare at 2:30 in the morning, and on the other side of it a group of dancers was boarding a cab. "Wait up," Amanda called to them—to be worth it, her death would have to look like an accident—and as a few eyed her with malice, she waved at them, then flew on her heels into the lights.

TORTURING
CREATURES AT
NIGHT

LAWN CLIPPINGS COVER ME LIKE TINY HAIRS. I'M LYING ON my stomach on the side of Mr. Mallak's house, watching him take apart a small engine in his basement. Whenever I watch someone in the neighborhood through a window well, I think about the possibility of poisonous spiders and keep my face a safe distance above the hole. Mr. Mallak has just unscrewed the starter plate and shroud of what I recognize to be a two-cycle Wisconsin Robin. It belongs to one among his fleet of remote-control Fokkers, of which there are parts all over his workshop, rudders and chassis, wing and tail assemblies, landing gear and propeller blades. He disconnects the spark plug lead, pops the oil drain plug on the crankcase, lets the thick syrup seep into a plastic coffee cup. Mr. Mallak is a retired psychiatrist, a specialist in the field of deviant behavior types. For two years he's been trying to get me to go with him to the parking lot of Marathon Picnic Area, to dogfight his crazy planes. Like a kid trying to get another kid to come outside and play, he knocks on the door at nine o'clock on a Saturday morning, asks me if I feel like being Baron von Richthofen for a couple of hours. No thanks, I tell him. He says he'll take the de Havilland D. H. 12, less sturdy though harder to see than the bright red Albatross D III he'll let me fly. Maybe next week, I tell him. The problem is, I'm twenty-seven, live with my father in a house on East Hill, and because I have no ostensible means of income, he thinks I'm ill.

I'm fat, over three hundred pounds fat, but I'm not ill. On this particular evening, I've got the remote control to my father's 27-inch Magnavox in my back pocket. I'm on the lookout for living rooms lit up like 1920s shadowgraphs—that is, for people watching TV. So far it's been a slow night. The Wilkes, who also own a Magnavox, left this morning in their Caravan, their rear piled so high with sleeping bags and fishing poles Mr. Wilke nearly backed over his mailbox. They'll be gone one week. Dr. Bednarski, who lives in the white bungalow with black shutters across the street, was watching a crime show, but his system is a Sony and incompatible. I crawl away from Mr. Mallak's window well, determined to find action somewhere on the block. I lift the latch on his gate quietly, step into the alley with enough surety to convince even the Rainville's bull terriers that I'm only Mr. Mallak out for a stroll, and they keep their mouths shut.

I take in Mr. Hartwig's prize Versailles rosebushes with my nose, as well as people's garbage. It's 10:45 on a cloudless night, and I'm excited because at eleven the Late Movie comes on on channel 12. Tonight it's *Frogs*, starring Ray Milland and Sam Elliot, in which a Fourth of July family picnic is interrupted by plotting reptiles and amphibians, a movie I think everyone should see at least once. The Pauls' kitchen light is on, I see from the alley, which means only that Mr. and Mrs. Paul have tucked in their six-month-old daughter Gayle and gone to bed. On the other side of the alley live the Ruechels, a house of six boys I have so far been able to avoid. Beyond the dark wall, which in daylight is a spirea hedge, my best friend from high school, Jess Roeder, appears to be throwing a party. Though I know it will depress me, I enter his backyard between two Norway pines and a newly planted dogwood, feel the cool spray on my face and arms from the sprinkler system next door, and crawl up to the shingled siding of a renovated early 1900s three-story Colonial. Jess is a month and three days younger than I am, yet is married to a Minneapolis girl named Lorna, has been to law school at Drake, owns a house featured each December in our city council's Tour of Homes.

You are ten. Your father sets the can of Black Flag down on the grass, calls you over to the window well in the back of your house. "There, son, is a black widow spider." You kneel on the lawn looking into the hole above your basement window, at the ribbed siding arched outward against the earth, at the collage of darkened leaves, at the chipped and encrusted window casement. In the corner sits the blue Superball you lost months ago when you slammed it as hard as you could against the driveway, watched it soar into the sky like a rebounding particle from space. You searched every inch of the yard for that ball, now there it is, looking newer, bluer somehow, than the day you forked over all the change in your pocket except a nickel and six pennies to the beige-faced lady behind the counter. You don't see the black widow immediately; it is as small and dark as the blind spot of an eye.

I don't really envy Jess Roeder, I think, as I plant my high-tops in the granite pebbles next to the house and try not to crush any of the boughs of two carpet junipers situated side by side beneath the electric meter. I'm to the right of the bay window, looking in at a kitchen table covered with assorted chips and snack dips. There's samba music coming through the window screen. I hear the voices of men whose pinstriped midsections are visible from the kitchen counter up and from the oak cabinets down. I recognize Jesse by his slim frame, so different from my own, and by the sureness of his manner of speaking, also different from my own. He and what I take to be his colleagues are talking about mechanics at the Imported Auto Garage on Highway 29, telling each other about the times they were soaked for routine body work, oil changes, tire rotations. My father has always driven Volvos, which he takes to Horak's Shell on Third Avenue for servicing. I crouch on all fours, crawl along the cement foundation over purple-leaf barberries and potentillas, to the downspout which marks the corner. As I stand I note that I am within six inches of being as tall as a full-grown pyramidal arborvitae and just as wide.

I cut through a vegetable garden to the white stucco Tudor owned by Judge Thomas and his wife Celia, see the shadows on the south side of the house, see the judge's fifteen-year-old daughter Becky and three of her girlfriends lying on sleeping bags in front of the set. It's a Zenith but with a remote-control detector the same frequency as the Magnavox at home. I hold the command to the window, punch in 12 so that it shows up on the television's channel indicator, press ENTER, and watch an MTV interview cut to a scene from *Frogs*.

"Why'd you change the station?" demands Becky Thomas's red-haired friend, a girl with cupids covering her pink pajamas.

"I didn't." Becky is a dark-haired girl I have admired from a distance since she was six.

"Neither did I," says a tall blonde girl clad in nothing but a light blue men's button-down shirt. "The remote control's way over there," she says, pointing one of her long, sun-tanned legs at the corner next to the wall.

On the screen is the scene near the beginning of the movie in which Kenneth is locked in a greenhouse with a Gila monster and fifty or sixty bearded lizards. Together they push over a jar of Malathion, another of 2,4-D, and the fumes rising from the toxic chemicals cause Kenneth to slump to the floor. "This is so stupid," says the red-headed girl. The blonde crawls over the thighs of a smaller blonde girl with glasses, who is wearing only a bra and a pair of men's white boxer shorts, picks up the remote control and points it at the set.

"Flip it back where it was," says the girl in boxer shorts, and I watch the screen scramble past fifteen different programs until she finds MTV. But I am undaunted. I believe these girls need to see this movie. I punch in 12, press ENTER, and *zap*, we see Kenneth's body on the floor of the greenhouse covered with lizards, the Gila monster inching forward to finish him off.

"God," says the red-headed girl. "It did it again."

"This is weird, you guys," says the thin blonde, sliding back inside her sleeping bag.

"Try punching 21," says Becky Thomas, but this time I cancel the blonde's command with my own remote control before she has a chance to enter it on the set, and my program stays on.

"It's not working," she says.

"Let me try it," Becky says. She punches 21, but as soon as I see it on the indicator, I press CANCEL, and again my program wins out. "I don't know," she says at last.

"I'm getting weirded," says the thin blonde.

"Yeah," says the red-headed girl, "me too."

Then Becky Thomas surprises me. She comes right up to the

window in her T-shirt and yellow underwear, says, "Tommy Pass? You out there?" I duck below the window. I am not Tommy Pass, though as I look at her heart-shaped mouth and necklace of pink beads, I can't help wishing that I were. Her cheeks are flushed; she wants Tommy Pass to be there on the other side of the metal screen, crouched below the window, huddled next to the chimney of white painted bricks. "He did this once before, you guys. He came to the window when I was watching TV and changed the station with his remote control." The crickets are chirping, but I am so near the judge's daughter I can hear her breathe. "I'm going out there," she says, and I see the excitement in her eyes. I hear the sliding glass door being unlocked, the heavy pane grating on the aluminum runner. I lie on my stomach behind a blue spruce, watch the girl come around the corner of the house. At night my black pants and T-shirt blend with the lawn. The girl looks right at me, right at the fat flesh of my face, but sees only a light spot under the tree, a beige bed of pine needles and dead grass.

"I see where he was standing," she says to her friends. She is standing barefoot outside the window, examining the indentations left by my shoes in the tall grass next to the house.

"How big are his feet?" asks the tall blonde. She has come to the window.

"Big," says Becky Thomas. In the warm night, I smell her sweet perfume.

"Maybe it's not him," says the blonde.

"Don't say that."

"Well, maybe it's not."

Becky Thomas bends over, presses the crumpled blades with her palms. That's when I realize my shoes have left prints in the lawn from the window to the blue spruce. She looks right at me, only this time I think she sees me. "Tommy Pass? If that's you, you better come out from behind that tree." She doesn't want to believe there's a strange fat man underneath the spruce, a spruce she watched her father plant, which works to my advantage. "Tom?" she calls out. "Tom Pass."

She takes a step forward. I hold my breath, keep my bloated body still. At this point, a blink could be fatal. "Yeah," I hear, and my head jerks against a low-hanging bough, but it's okay because she, too, has heard the husky voice of a boy beyond the spirea hedge. "Tommy," she says.

"Hey Beck," says the boy, who comes up behind me on the newly sprinkled lawn. His work boots land on either side of my protuberant sneakers, the soles of which I painted black for just this situation. He sees me, I'm sure of it, but he doesn't say a word. I watch him greet Becky. He notices her T-shirt and yellow underwear, touches her white cheek with the side of his hand. "What're you doing out?" he asks her, taking her hand in his.

"As if you didn't know." She places his hand on her nyloned hip, wraps her long white arms around his neck.

"I was out on the street and I heard my name."

"You mean," says Becky Thomas, "after you left the window."

"What?"

"The window." She motions with her head at the window into the living room.

"I wasn't out terrorizing," he says, "if that's what you mean." He pushes her away, his long lean arms dangling at his sides like billy clubs. "Who are you really waiting for? Sully? Barbie? You know, Beck, the guys at school have been talking. Your name's come up a few times." The boy named Tommy Pass puts his hands into his pockets as if loose they might start swinging of their own accord, do more damage than he ever intended. "You really disappoint me," he says, a phrase I suspect he has taken from his father.

As I listen to their conversation, I long to hold the child in my corpulent arms, press her to my breast, assure her that she needn't fear disappointing anyone, not herself, and other people least of all. "I haven't seen Sully or Barbie," she says. "I'm having a slumber party. Missy Jaeks, Mona Peterson, and Carol Bautsch are over."

"Mona Peterson?"

"Yeah. She'll tell you the story. The television set kept switching to this frog movie."

"Really?" he asks. "Did Mona think I did it, too."

"I don't know," Becky Thomas says. "Why would she?"

"How should I know?" says Tommy Pass. "All right, I'll come in for a little while."

"Where is it?" you ask your father, and he points at it with the can of insect spray. Cobwebs droop from the window casements like the negligees you have seen on his closet door. Dried-out dead spiders hang from the jambs and sashes, their tiny legs crippled as arthritic fingers. The black widow is perched on top of a brown egg sac, there where your father points the aerosol spray tip, suspended in space on a web beading with wetness. A wonder you haven't seen it straight off. Perhaps you expected it to be hiding underneath the top rail of the window or in one of the long cracks in the weather stripping. Instead it is about six inches below the rounded lip of corrugated metal, its legs sprawled out like the veins of a leaf, its body bloated like a pustule of ink. It is still, except for its pedipalpi, which hold a fly.

Becky Thomas leads Tommy Pass around the corner of the house, and I shove the remote control back in my hip pocket. I stand up, trembling. From now on, I tell myself, I'll have to avoid Judge Thomas's house, at least when his daughter is watching. Even if she doesn't understand the physics behind infrared radiation, she knows there's nothing supernatural about channels changing at night. I step into the Thomas's front yard, and as I pass the lamp post, I hear voices belonging to Tommy Pass's friends. They are standing at the end of the driveway, a group of six or seven, all wearing yellow Hornet letter jackets. I dart out of the light, but it's too late. A congenitally chubby boy, who will no doubt be as fat as I am by age twenty, sees me and says to the others, "It's Fig Newton. You see him? He cut into the front yard of Sweeny's old house."

"Big Fig?"

"Positive. Saw him."

I am back in Jess Roeder's yard, on the side of the house, running as fast as I can across the lawn, a blancmange flung into the night. My weight, far from slowing me down, gives me momentum. Behind me, I hear the snapping of nine-bark branches, the crack of a newly planted tree hydrangea; the boys are crashing after me. One day in third grade, a kid named Layne Eggers nicknamed me after the Nabisco fruit bar, and for eighteen years the name has stuck. About twenty yards behind me, a boy hurls "Fig Newton" at me like a QB passing a football on the scramble. "Hey Fig-Face!" he yells. At the edge of the back lawn, I tip over some garbage cans in the alley, hoping to trip them up on the other side of the spirea hedge. These boys may be faster than I am, but I know this neighborhood like a skin graft. I barrel down the alley, cut back through Mr. Hartwig's trellises of *pompon de Paris*, duck under a wire clothesline, not because I see it, but because from experience I know it's there. Cutting across his cement porch, I hear the clank of shins on metal, the boys meeting the trash can obstacle. "He went thatta way," I hear one of them say, "into Hartwig's yard." I'm on the driveway when one of the boys ensnares himself in rose vines, then another catches his neck in the clothesline. As I cross Fulton Street three boys come out from behind a blue Pontiac, two others down the block a little way, close to the high school. "There he is!" one of them says. I'm in Mrs. Bolte's backyard now and know exactly where I'm going to hide.

When the first yellow jacket rounds the corner of the house, I'm lying on my stomach on two bags of compost, wedged in between Mrs. Bolte's two-car garage and screened atrium. "This is where he went," says one of the boys, scanning the area between the foundation of the house and a landscaped mound of bark.

"Maybe he jumped the fence," says another.

"That tub?"

"You see him anywhere!"

"That doesn't mean he isn't here."

There are only three boys now. I watch them split up to cover the lawn. A dark-haired boy with track medals takes the porch, checks underneath the chaise longue and redwood-stained picnic table. The two blond-haired boys move out of my field of view, but I can hear their legs in Mrs. Bolte's dianthums and leadwarts, hear them shaking her mock orange and Russian sage. When they get to the clumps of chest-high pussy willows along the back rail of her picket fence, they kick the brittle stalks and snap them in half like straws. One of the boys topples her cement birdbath. I hear the splash of water on grass, the cracking of the bath against its pedestal. I detest such needless destruction, though I understand its impulse. "You in there, Fig?" says one of the blond-haired boys. "Come on out, Figgy."

"You think he ditched us?"

"Looks that way." The two blond-haired boys come back into view. The taller of the two stares up the trunk of a honey locust, a thin-branched tree which in winter can barely support the weight of snow.

"You think he's up there, Corey?"

"Sure, Waldo-ski," he says.

"Let's get out of here."

"Pass is probably palucking Becky Thomas."

"You think so?"

"He's done it before."

"You want your ball?" your father asks, but before you can answer, he fires the death spray at the black widow spider, coating its body with a fine white sheen. The spider, leaving its egg sac dripping in the center of the web, scrambles straight into the blast like a kamikaze. You watch it climb onto the lip of corrugated metal. Your father holds the can an inch away from its tiny head. The yellow eye of death looms in each of its eight. Your father says, "Pay attention, son." He presses the button again. This time the spider bounces into the air, and from the edge of the web, mortally poisoned, it eyes you. It tries to straighten itself out, but its legs curl under it like singed hairs. Your father lets it crawl onto the grass. It no longer radiates panic. It wants simply to be left alone. Your father flips it so its orange hourglass faces the sky. Then he presses it into the earth with the rim of the can until its body breaks in half and white fluid seeps from its cephalothorax.

The boys take off like deer, but I wait about ten minutes before leaving my cover. Out from between the garage and the house, I notice lights on in Mrs. Bolte's basement, so I crawl over grass and cedar chips to her window well, plant my belly in the center of her coiled garden hose. The window is a double-hinge, open about four inches, and Mrs. Bolte is sitting on a velveteen Barcalounger in front of a Magnavox the same model as my father's. A gray woman in her sixties, she was my World Lit teacher in high school the year her husband died of a lymphosarcoma. She is watching a church service on one of the Christian networks when I take out my remote control and flip the channel to *Frogs*, entertainment more worth her while than fire-and-brimstone televangelism. It's the scene in the movie in which Maybelle, an eccentric butterfly collector, is pursued down a boggy path by Florida 'gators and winds up tripping on her dress into leech-infested quicksand. When the scene comes on, Mrs. Bolte cranks the handle on the recliner and sits bolt upright.

She punches in her channel, but I pull the CANCEL routine and the two of us watch Maybelle attempt to climb out of the swamp, her fleshy face and arms dripping with black leeches. Mrs. Bolte spars with me only once. When the scene shifts to the drawing room of Jason Crockett, the game-hunting patriarch played by Ray Milland, Mrs. Bolte leaves her chair with the conviction of a believer. I assume she's going to turn off the set, amuse herself with some epic poetry, but when she walks past the television altogether, I realize she's got something else in mind. She takes a black box the size of a Monopoly game off the top shelf of her bookcase, unhooks a crucifix from the panelled wall, sets both on the end table next to her chair. Meanwhile, the only character who knows what's going on, Pickett Smith, is shuffling people off the island through a jungle laden with anacondas and puff adders, iguanas and poisonous leopard frogs.

Mrs. Bolte takes a Ouija board out of its box, unfolds it on her lap, sets the wooden crucifix carefully on the alphabet, her fingers resting on the plaster-of-Paris Jesus as if on the home keys of an antique typewriter. "Benny," she says, "I feel your presence in the room with me tonight. In the walls and in my bones. Dear heart, I want you to talk to me. Flip the stations around. We'll watch whatever you want to tonight—*Dr. Jekyll and Mr. Hyde*, *Invasion of the Body Snatchers*—but I want you to tell me how you are. Are your joints causing you pain?" I see the crucifix move across the board under her painted nails, see the curled feet of Jesus point to the N in the upper right-hand corner. "No, I wouldn't imagine they would be. You were a martyr, a real martyr. Anything else you want to tell me? You were always such a marvelous speller."

Jesus' feet scuttle over to the I, to the L, the O, and V. "That's all very fine," Mrs. Bolte says. I see the corner of one eye fill with water. "Don't spell it out. I love you, too. Only now it's cold and rarefied, like the love one has for a great old poem. God, oh, God," she says. She looks at the pane of glass, and for a second I think she sees me, but her eyes are glazed, and the wrinkles on her forehead arch into perfect temples. At this point she could be seeing just about anything in the sheen I lurk behind, even Benny. She turns her face to the board. "Harold Lindstrom came by yesterday. You should have seen how he admired the pussy willows you planted that Veterans' Day. He said he was thinking of doing up his yard the same way. Now I told him he could have the birdbath. Not the precious one, never that one. The one in the garage, sweetheart. Tell me you don't mind."

But Benny is reluctant to tell her much of anything. The crucifix sweeps back and forth across the board like the needle of a radio tuner. Only there's no sound but the croaking of frogs, and I begin to think maybe the two really are communicating. "I knew it," she says. "Now you're angry." This is a bit too much for me. I believe in an indifferent universe. So with fifteen minutes left in the movie, I punch 45, press ENTER, and watch the screen flip back to the evangelist and his blue-robed choir. "You don't want to watch this," Mrs. Bolte says. But I do not change the station. "Does this mean you're leaving?" I put the remote control back in my hip pocket as Jesus edges to the side of the board like a wind-up toy that's running down. It's over. I'm not doing this anymore, I tell myself, as Jesus drops off like dead weight between Mrs. Bolte and the armrest.

"Fudge," she says.

Your father wipes off the bottom of the can with his handkerchief, then empties the can onto the tiny egg sac. "Don't want the progeny running around," he says, and you kneel in the grass for a long time looking at the black widow severed on the grass, at the dark bud on the green lawn.

When I reach the front yard of my house, I check the garage to see whether my father is home yet. He's not, which is fine with me. He's a proctologist with a penchant for nurses, who has since the day of my mother's funeral expected me to be as smooth with the ladies as he is. But I have never been smooth with anyone. Jess Roeder is the only friend I've ever had. Inside, I lock the front door, switch off the porch light, and slam my hands as hard as I can on the oak balustrade down the steps to the basement. In my bedroom, I put *Life in a Cage* onto the turntable and listen to my favorite guitarist of all time blast out his brains on a Hagstrom-Swede. I take off my black T-shirt and elastic pants and throw them onto the heap in my closet. I take Herman Munster out of his terrarium, lie naked on my unmade bed, and let the Mojave brown tarantula crawl around on my blubbery flesh. In this country, tarantulas must have their venom glands removed by an arachnologist before they may be legally sold in pet shops, but sometimes their fangs are also removed. Before I forked over the hundred and fifty dollars for my tarantula, I made the pet shop owner show me both of its pitch-black teeth. Herman Munster lowers his abdomen to my rib cage, pulls in his legs like loaded springs, and pounces catlike onto my left breast. He sinks his fangs into the flesh below my nipple, then scrambles backward into the tufts of brown hair as if proud of the new pink welt he's left.

I hear the motor of the electric garage door, then the footsteps of my father on the stairs to the basement. Behind them like an echo are footsteps which could belong to either Lorraine Lodgekins or Colleen Burns. I turn off the lamp beside my bed, pull the sheets over Herman and me. My father opens the door to my bedroom just a crack, and a strip of light from the hall crosses the side of my face. Without opening my eyes I know that it is Miss Lodgekins who is with him.

"Dennis is asleep," my father says.

"Good," says Miss Lodgekins.

"I look at him, and I want to cry," my father says.

"Come on," she says.

Miss Lodgekins closes the door and dissolves the screen inside my head. Under the covers, Herman Munster sinks his fangs into my belly. I try to push him off with my hand, and his scopulae drag across my side. As I roll over he scurries across my back, down my legs to the end of the bed where he will spend the night, reposed between my feet. Falling asleep, I wonder what I'll say to Mr. Mallak when he knocks on the door tomorrow morning at nine and asks to speak to the Baron von Richthofen.

I'M IN THE AIR IN THE COCKPIT OF AN ALBATROSS D III, A Sopwith Camel off my left wing tip. I pull back on the flap levers, crank the control yoke hard right, and aim my machine gun at the shiny fuselage above me. The pilot pulls back on the thrust lever and arches his plane to the left, a maneuver I have anticipated with the front and rear sights of my machine gun. I jam in the operating rod, press the firing lever with my thumb, but no bullets come out. The cartridge box isn't feeding properly. The other pilot lowers his plane to my level. I look into the dark eye of his flash suppressor. Shortly, I know, he will spray me with fire.

make plans, but only the ones I make count. I click off and leave my room with the riveting posters of animal sacrifices, goats dipped in kerosene and torched, rabbits gutted and thrown to the hungry mobs, neither of which have I had the opportunity to witness with my own eyes! About the best muzick to pass through this pleasant Wisconsin town was over a year ago now, some happy-go-lucky kids who called themselves Abortion, *not* The Abortion, or Abor*tions*, but Abortion, singular, without an article, which in a humorous way is more graphic (and therefore better!) than many of the names musical groups came up with in the past, names beginning with "The," or worse, pluralized. But, to be honest, the group in question was not all that different from many other groups current or defunct, which is to say, there was nothing that uniquely charming about them, which is to say that while their name was inspired, their poster is not on my wall!

Down the hall, where the charger for the phone is located, my own parent (her name is Candice) appears to be whipping up some of her own bomb material out of the scraps of yesterday's pig, some cheddar filings, and two cups of elbow macaroni. "Allow me, Mother," I say. She is the most terrific parent a boy like me could wish for, and I use every opportunity to make her feel wanted.

"Would you?" she says. I take the wooden spoon from her hand *gladly*, because I know she has a lot to do in preparation for her date with Harold W. Lindstrom, M.D., who is more or less her boss, and with whom she has been fascinated since before her divorce from my other parent, Don. She is quite an attractive woman, I would say, despite her age (which is 38!), and I like her mostly for the active interest she takes in me and my doings. As always she is frank with me about her plans for the evening and tells me the name of the restaurant where Harold W. Lindstrom,

M.D., has made their dinner reservations (Geribaldi's on Rural Route K) and even writes down the telephone numbers where she may be reached in case of an emergency (824-7658 and 234-0223, respectively). She asks me whether I'm doing anything with Jon, which is not a name Semen, a.k.a. Meloche, goes by very often, but I understand whom she means well enough to answer, "Yes," and add, "we're thinking of attending the girls' gymnastics meet tonight. They're competing against those limber girls from Rothschild." Which is far from being a lie since Semen and I have thought quite a lot about the girls' gymnastics meet, and what's more, the girls from Rothschild *are* limber, especially one, whom you will meet shortly, once this true-to-life account has had a chance to unfold! Candice (my parent) winks at me and laughs, as if she can see in the twinkle of my eye the girl about whom Semen has had dreams (the thin, dark-haired gymnast whom you will shortly meet, whose name is Mona!), but I don't tell her, which is quite a different thing than lying! that what's causing my eyes to twinkle is the thought of Christmas lights, which is to say, all those cozy homes bedecked with bulbs.

"Honestly, you're becoming so mature," she says, which *is* the truth when one considers the kind of person I was a year ago, before I started hearing the words of artists like Blood Spot, Lung Wound, and Sexual Knifing, and many others whom I will mention as the need arises—a person living in fear, afraid to leave the house, afraid to go to school, afraid to enter the world about which the aforementioned recording stars sing so poignantly! "We're like roommates," she says, and she's right, we are! which is another reason I like and respect her so much and try never to miss an opportunity to make her feel wanted. Which is *not* how it is with other of my friends, like Semen for instance, whose parents come down

awfully hard on him at times, like when he comes home an hour
late from a girls' gymnastics meet, or just comes home late.

In just her bathrobe, she leaves the bomb manufacturing center of the house we share, with its jars of oatmeal, millet, flour, its
tins of spices and herbs, its pantry of canned fruits and vegetables
and refrigerator of eggs, catsup, mayonnaise, and cottage cheese!
To be honest, as her hips sway past the trestle table on which, to
date, perhaps a hundred bombs have been constructed! I see the
raw sexuality men have found so attractive, and I am happy for her
that she is unlike all the other parents I have ever met, like Semen's
for instance, who has emaciated herself with diet pills, or Le
Chefski's, who is a pig. And thinking about how nice it is to be able
to see Candice so clearly, without any of the emotional coloring I
have noticed in other kids' descriptions of their progenitors, I
strain the macaroni in a colander, add a tablespoon of milk, stir in
the hog bits and cheddar filings, and dump it all into a bag.

I wash the equipment in the sink and put it away in the cup-
boards because I know there is nothing as irritating to a parent,
even one as happy-go-lucky as mine! as a counter covered with
used dishes. I walk down the hallway to her bedroom (she doesn't
insist on my knocking before entering, and doesn't care if I see her
nude, which I have many times! because she has a very nice body
for a thirty-eight-year-old woman, and she should be proud of it!),
but she is nowhere to be seen because she is in the bathroom show-
ering for her date with Harold W. Lindstrom, M.D. I open the
bathroom door and call to her through the beveled glass until she
turns off the water on the Shower Massage, which I can imagine
making her normally large nipples even more swollen and erect
and red (because I have seen them in that state many times!). "I'm
leaving now, Mother. Thank you so much for starting the delicious

macaroni and cheese with ham chunks. You always know just how to please a boy like me by thinking of his tremendous appetite."

"You're welcome, Tommy," she says, addressing me by the most formal of my three names. People who know me kind of well call me Pass, because it's my last name, but people who know me really well call me Penis, because it's another P word (like Pass!), but mostly because of my own penis's monstrous size! "Have fun," she says.

"I want you in by ten o'clock," I say. "I'll be checking my watch every fifteen minutes."

She laughs, which is another of her many wonderful qualities. Were I thirty-eight myself and not related to her biologically, it would be her laugh, which is hollow and deep and as melodic as an oboe (which is *not* an instrument I am inordinately fond of ordinarily!), that would make me hard, which it kind of does anyway even though I am not thirty-eight and *am* very much related to her biologically in my role as son. In the entryway to the great outdoors, I put on my World War II paratrooper's jacket, which Candice purchased for me at my request from the two very articulate and humorous old men who operate the war novelties shop that our city council is trying to push out of the pedestrian mall and into Harris Machinery, which is an abandoned brick building with busted windows five blocks away from any other merchant. It (the jacket!) cost $350 but luckily had a number of important selling points, one of which is the authentic .35 caliber machine-gun holes (three) in a diagonal across the front and back, and second (the clincher as far as Candice was concerned) a thermal lining unsurpassed for warmth. Lucky for them (the two old men, whose names are Milty and Ak!), they have me living in this city with them, or else many of their highly descriptive and often amusing narratives of heinous war crimes and youthful debauchery would go unheard by anyone except them. I, with only limited access to funds my other parent (Don) makes available to our (now) two-atom molecular family, do everything I can to keep those two old men in business, which means buying their stock whenever opportunity allows, by which I mean swastikas, Iron Crosses, and army-issue knives that are spring-loaded and thus for display purposes only.

I pack the food at the bottom of the bag until it is a highly compressed, snowball-sized core and seal the bomb with a twisty. Then I place it carefully at the bottom of one of my jacket's huge side pockets (another of its selling points! when Candice was thinking of dividing the $350 between a piece of winter clothing and a heavy-duty backpack for books). Soon I am out in the neighborhood admiring all the red, yellow, and green bulbs flickering on the snow-layered eaves and lawns, on my way to the cul-de-sac on top of East Hill, where one night each June the frogs parade en masse and where, without much further ado, this adventurous and action-packed tale of blood-curdling horror has its beginning. Semen is waiting for me under the street lamp, a chop suey bomb dangling between his legs, which he opens up and shows me, and so I open up my bomb for him, and for several long and pleasurable seconds we allow ourselves to be riveted by the thought of such desirable shrapnel—water chestnuts and macaroni, mushroom sauce and ham. I say, "Shall we get to the business at hand?" and he says, "I do believe it's time." Then we walk up the driveway to the porch of a two-story Dutch colonial.

On the other side of some very lovely taffeta curtains, a television is being watched, the volume turned up high, gunshots ricocheting from the cozy firelit world of eggnog and naps into the cold, neon-lit world of intrigue. Semen balances across the upper rail of the balustrade like a cat burglar—he could've been a gymnast!—unscrewing bulbs that would scorch his fingers to raisins were it not for the thick, heat-resistant gloves we wear. While he works the entablature, I fill my pockets with bulbs from pine trees that punctuate the intercolumnation like a series of Spanish exclamations. "¡Bombas como frutas! ¡Bombas como nueces!" We strip the cords of lights in less time than it takes a station to break, then move to the split-level ranch next door where we harvest another twenty-five bulbs from a wreath hung below the transom. "How many do you have?" I ask.

"Sixty or seventy," Semen says.

"Let's make it an even hundred apiece," I say, and so we do, with bulbs from a geodesic dome at the end of a long wooded drive. Then we cut through the trees, cross Rural Route J, and take cover between the placard of Saint Alban's Episcopal Church and a fifteen-foot monolithic cross behind it. As Acuras, Mercedeses, and BMWs leave the church parking lot, we arc handfuls of light-bulb bombs over the sign and watch them explode on the shiny roofs and hoods. It is a spectacular sight, one for which Semen and I have waited nearly eleven months, and it is not a letdown. Very few experiences in life are as long as you don't romanticize them into experiences they aren't, which is to say, Semen and I have remembered everything accurately—the pops! the sparks and flickers of globes impacting on metal. Every so often, a car stops, a door opens, but these are people dressed for mass, who are not about to risk life and limb in a high-speed foot chase over snow, through woods and cornfields. Which is precisely why, when our arsenals have dwindled to fifty or sixty bulbs, we leave off for a while in expectation of more athletic enemy.

"Think we'll hook into some danger?" Semen asks.

"Be patient," I say. We sit in the snow, smoking fags, till the last congregant has pulled from the lot.

"Ready for some danger?" Semen asks. We stand up, each with a handful of bombs, as a car comes up the hill with its high beams on, doing about sixty. We hurl about fifteen bombs over the sign before I even see that it is a blue Chrysler Le Baron. Explosions occur in front of it, behind it, and on it in a shower of pelts and sparks. "Direct hit!" Semen says. The driver slams on his breaks, which is what we have been waiting for, but the person who emerges from the car is none other than Harold W. Lindstrom, M.D.

"We gotta run!"

I grab Semen's throat and whisper into his hair, "Stay calm."

Harold W. Lindstrom, M.D., steps onto the snow in his black wingtips with the slick leather soles. Through a knot in the wood, I see the collar of Candice's lynx stole, her pulled-back hair, one dangling gold earring. "The shenanigans are over," he says as Candice purses her lips together in the light of the vanity mirror. "So you might as well come out and show yourselves." I hear Semen's frenetic fearful breathing at my shoulder, which is a shame, for he cannot see the pale draining of potency from the face of Harold W. Lindstrom, M.D., nor enjoy the power of our concealment in the brittle network of shrubbery. "You can't fool me," says Harold W. Lindstrom, M.D., "I know you're behind there." His eyes are not on the sign, but on the huge, monolithic cross rising behind it. He takes a step backward as Candice lowers the electronic window.

"Come on, Harold," she says.

The wind flicks up his thin, gray hair. Gray vapors rise from his mouth and nostrils. "Whoever they are, they need help."

"You don't even know where they are," she says.

"They're behind the sign." He points at us. "They're in between the sign and the cross."

"How do you know?"

"It's where the bulbs came from. The jerks threw Christmas bulbs at us." He swings his arms. "We could have gotten into an accident. You know who'd be called from the hospital? Hedda, that's who."

Candice parts her lips in an expression of raw sexuality. "I saw them running," she says. "Dressed in black. They're behind the church by now, probably hiding in a cornfield."

"You saw them running?"

"Before you even stopped the car. Come on, Harold, we're late as it is."

He walks back to the car and inspects the finish. He runs his hand over the roof and raises his fist at us. "You're sick kids! You hear me? You ought to be locked up!" As he gets back in the car I ease up on Semen's head, which has been like a nut in a cracker throughout the whole ordeal. Semen rubs his neck as the blue Chrysler Le Baron bears Candice and her date out of town going to a place I have only heard about, Geribaldi's, where the waiters wear tuxedos, where the diners wash their fingers in tiny bowls and they serve a 1977 vintage that Candice could not afford were it not for Harold W. Lindstrom, M.D., and the money he has made as an obstetrician and gynecologist. To be honest I am thrilled for her, because my other parent (Don) was only the head mechanic at an imported auto garage and could only afford to take her to places like the Wagon Wheel Family Restaurants on Water Street and on East Franklin.

"Your mother is something else," Semen says.

"I know it," I say.

"I wish my parents would divorce," he says.

"Maybe they will," I offer half-heartedly because I know they won't. Semen and I expend the rest of our bulbs on passing traffic. A college kid chases us into the playground behind the church, and a little later a police officer chases us into a cornfield. We outwait him, our stomachs pressed to the frozen stalks, then we walk back to the road and stand on the shoulder for a car to come and receive our food bombs. Semen and I are not prone to lapses of nostalgia, but as we are standing there on the snow and gravel, our bombs dangling at our sides like hobo sacks, Semen asks me whether I think it will be a good frog season, and I ask him what he means by "good."

"Will there be a lot of them?" he asks. "A lot of frogs?"

I tell him there's no way to know until the night of the parade.

"Last year," he says, "there were a lot of frogs. They came out four nights after the full moon. Also, it was after a winter of barely any snow. This winter there's a lot of snow. I wonder if that means they'll come out on the full moon, or maybe even before it. What if this year they come out in late May, before the end of school? If they came out on a school night, we might miss them altogether. Then the whole next year we'd be thinking that, if we had another winter with lots of snow, it would mean they wouldn't be coming out at all."

"That could never happen," I say.

"Why not?" Semen asks.

"Because if they paraded on a school night, we'd see a few of the squished ones on the street the next day. And we would know that a winter with snow doesn't mean a summer night without frogs."

And for a long time it seemed as if anybody who was going anywhere had gotten there and that Semen and I might have to wait hours for them to return.

IN THIS GREAT WORLD, I BELIEVE WITH SLIT MEMBRANE, Stomach Tumor, and Infected Gash that it doesn't pay to feel anything but glad, for, in the words of the late Thomas Jefferson (the lead singer of Cut, who shot himself in the head with a Saturday Night Special while performing in Philadelphia!), "How ever bad it gets, there's still no telling whose guts you'll see on the pavement tomorrow!" And it's true, at least in a metaphorical sense, for no sooner have I begun to sing the lyrics from the title track of Cut's album, *Fatal Surgery* (****1/2), than Semen and I see headlights at the bottom of East Hill. Each of us palms his bomb, and when the car (which reveals itself to be a cream-colored Mustang with drags) crests the top, Semen and I lob our sacks in front of it. Food explodes off the windshield. The car swerves to a stop, which forces us into the woods across the street from the church, where we look on from within the shadows of branches and tree trunks. "Know what?" I say, "I think we just nailed Le Chefski's brother's car."

"No," says Semen.

"Yes," I say, "I think we did." The Mustang rests there cocked on the shoulder, its headlights blazing into a cornfield, its taillights pulsing in time with our temples. We should run, we know, especially if it *is* Le Chefski's brother, who is six-foot-three, nineteen years old, and crazier than either Semen or I, which is precisely why we don't, why we stand there in the copse, trying to see through the side window whose face exists behind the headrest, whose cheek is an otherworldly, dashboard green. "We might've hooked into some danger," I say, as the headlights blink off and the Mustang moves backward over the snow and gravel to the spot where Semen and I were standing when we lobbed our bombs. The inside of the car is now a cavern of darkness. The driver rolls down his window and out of it, like a probe, comes the long, black barrel of a shotgun (12-gauge!).

"Come on," says Semen, three trees away. "We gotta run!"

"Run and he'll pick you off like a turkey!"

"I don't care!" Semen's boots have already begun to crunch through the layers of icy crust. Fire flashes three times from the end of the barrel in such quick succession I hear only one blast. Snow drops from the upper limbs as Semen, who is hardly more substantial than a shadow, drops to his knees and then to his chest on the white ground. I move from tree trunk to tree trunk to where Semen lies in a huddled mass. "I'm hit," he says. It's dark, granted, but I don't see any blood. I take off my gloves and feel his body with my hands, starting at the head and working my way down to the boots.

"Where?" I ask him.

"I'm not sure."

"Come on," I urge him. "Where?"

"I don't know!"

"Penis!" I look up and see Le Chefski himself standing on the gravel in front of the Mustang.

"Since when have you been old enough to drive?" I ask him.

"Since Wayne gave me the keys," Le Chefski says. He trudges out into the snow.

"Where've you been?" I ask.

"All over," he says. "The gymnastics meet. Looking for you. My brother's having a party."

"At the farm?"

"Yeah. My parents came to town for a weekend at the Holiday Inn."

"Semen says he's shot," I say.

"Naw he's not," says Le Chefski. "I fired over his head."

"Maybe I'm not," says Semen, sitting up. "It sure as hell felt like I was."

"You would be if I'd aimed at you," says Le Chefski. "But I didn't and that's why you're not. You want to come out to the farm? Mona's going to be there, but you better not mess with her, Pass. She's pissed at you."

"She pissed at you?" I ask.

"Yeah, she's pissed at me. She's pissed at Semen, too."

"But she said she was coming to the party. She said that to you?"

"Yeah."

"Why?" I ask.

"I don't know. I think she has a thing for my brother."

"Wayne?" I'm incredulous. Le Chefski's brother has been in eleventh grade for three years.

"She thinks he's nice."

"Him?"

"You want to come or not?"

"We're out of bombs," I say. So the three of us walk back to the road and get in the Mustang, me in the front and Semen in the back with the shotgun. Le Chefski works the wipers, and soon Rural Route J is flowing under our tires like a stream of hot black coffee. Mailboxes and fence posts bend and converge to points on either side of us, like liquids pushed through huge syringes, and I am thinking about Mona and what she will say to me and what I will say to her, about the group Nasty Abrasion, and the idea for the riveting pep fest skit that came to me while hearing the poetry of their greatest single, "Fetus in a Bag," off the *Buckets of Sperm* CD. In it (the song!) two lines are repeated for fifteen minutes and thirty-seven seconds.

My baby's got some death in her—
Got to find me a cellophane bag.

(©1996 Mutilated Muzick, Inc.)

Which gave me the vision of Semen dressed up as a pregnant Rothschild gymnast and Le Chefski as an abortionist! In it (the skit, performed this morning in the gym! before the screaming masses!) Le Chefski, wearing Mr. Johnson's white lab coat with a large W (our school letter!) emblazoned on his back, pushes Semen onto the basketball court in a red wheelbarrow. Mr. Morrel, our principal, is so relieved that someone has had the school spirit to put together a skit at all that he has decided to take a nap in his office—or so I assume from his absence at the fest! The kids, who are seated by grade level on the bleachers, are screaming, "Kill Rothschild! Kill the Rothschild gymnasts!" and for several long and pleasurable seconds, Le Chefski conducts them with a wire coat hanger, which he has bent into a baton and which, as a hush descends over the auditorium, he places between the spread knees of Semen, who is screaming in agony and shaking his long black wig better than he ever did in rehearsal! A number of teachers leave their seats and exit through the doors, which is their right! I hear Bunson, who is a kid we know, say "Go for it!" and I am glad, for it's kids like Bunson who would never think of showing their support for our talented girls were it not for us! A bunch of kids have clumped in front of the exits. I see Mr. Morrel's head hovering above the mob, on his face a scrunched-up look of consternation, which is one of the artistic effects we are trying to achieve! From a large grocery sack concealed in the folds of Semen's hospital robe, Le Chefski delivers the sickness for all to see, the metaphor for the Rothschild girls' notoriously bad performances season after season, which is to say, Le Chefski reaches into the paper sack and orchestrates a great eruption of war novelties from between Semen's spread thighs. I see Mr. Morrel stumble over McEntire's foot, which is in a cast from a skiing accident, as debris falls to the floor around Le Chefski, debris in the form of Nazi armbands, hand grenade casings, Iron Crosses, machine-gun shells, and spring-loaded knives! With an air of what can only be described as artistic snobbery, Mr. Morrel comes onto the gymnasium floor, grabs Semen and Le Chefski by the scruffs of their skinny necks, and takes them away to his office, where he gives them a lecture which lasts fifty-seven minutes by my watch.

At the intersection with Rural Route K, I see the sign for Geribaldi's ("Fine Dining. International Cuisine. Overlooking Phlox Lake. 8 Miles.") and imagine Candice seated across a candle-lit table from Harold W. Lindstrom, M.D., and so I ask Le Chefski if he has something to put in the deck besides country-western muzick, which are mainly songs about people cheating and being dishonest with one another, which I do not believe in. "Wayne listens to that death shit," Le Chefski says, "not me."

"He does?" I ask.

"Sure," says Le Chefski. "He's got tons of it. Bone. Skin and Spleen. Testosterone Catastrophe."

"He listens to Testosterone Catastrophe?" I ask.

"He goes to sleep to it," says Le Chefski.

"They're excellent," says Semen from the backseat. Le Chefski pulls the car onto a long gravel drive studded with pickups, Dusters, and El Caminos. Groups of older kids stand outside the house, their jackets and caps lit up by lights radiating from every window. Le Chefski parks the car outside the barn, next to the shiny green corn harvester which Le Chefski leaves school early every fall to operate. I let Semen out of the back and hear the unmistakable guitar noise of Grim Reaper, the brilliant founding member of the group Blood and Bile, whose first album, *I Want to Blow Your Head Off*, shook the American charts by challenging all prior musical conventions! We walk over the stamped-down snow to the house past kids smoking fags and drinking from plastic cups. Le Chefski leaves Semen and me standing in the living room, among kids who try to pretend we're not there (because we're ninth-graders!), but I have a friend in Grim Reaper, who speaks to kids like me, "Splatter! Fry! Splatter! Die!" Which is when I see Mona in the kitchen talking to Le Chefski's brother, Wayne.

She is wearing a black skirt and tights, her long black curls snaking down the back of her red letter jacket. "There she is," I say to Semen, who began dreaming about her the night I told him about her tongue, which was a week before Mona and I first fucked and caused Semen to fall head over heels in love. "I'm going to talk to her," I say to Semen, but when I get there it's Wayne I address. "This is a great party, Wayne," I say, interrupting his vivid and interesting account of pig slaughtering, which is what the Le Chefski family does when they aren't producing two of the world's all-time greatest bomb materials—milk and corn.

"Yeah? What's so great about it?" he challenges.

"The muzick!"

"Yeah?" His tone brightens.

"Yeah," I say. "Little Le Chefski tells me you listen to T.C. I've got all three of their albums, *Uncomfortable Womb*, *Organ Donor*, and *Amp U. T.*"

"*You* have *Amp U. T.*?"

"I had to order it from England. It's got 'Baring My Fang' on it. It's got '(Give Me an Axe) Let Me Be Your Butcher.' It's got 'Clot.'"

"'Clot'?" he says. I nod. It's a wonderful and riveting song about bleeding from a heart wound, which is why it is one of Semen's favorites. "God, I'd love to hear 'Clot' right now. You want to hear something off *Organ Donor*?"

"'Music Man,'" I say.

"I fucking *love* that song!" Wayne says.

"Put it on," I say.

"Mona, you wanna hear 'Music Man'?"

"Sure," she says, which is all it takes for Wayne to begin squeezing himself and his fifth of sour mash through the kitchen of bodies to the cabinet in the living room where the high-fidelity CD-player and tuner are located. Which is how it happens that I am left with Mona, who is also a ninth-grader and who (because she goes to Rothschild High School) knows even fewer of the people at the party than I do!

"Well, I guess I'm a little disappointed in you," I say, which I know is something her male parent, Herb, says to her quite often, because she has told me so (many times!).

"Now I've heard it all," she says, which is what Lois, her female parent, says whenever Herb tells her he's had to work after hours at the window plant, which employs a large portion of Rothschild's male *and* female populace. "If you expect me to forgive you, you can just forget it."

On the other side of the house, Wayne lifts the needle off Blood and Bile's "Tell It Like It Is," as two fat droplets collect on Mona's lower lashes, which are two good signs. "I'm not asking you to forgive me, Mona, because I haven't done anything wrong."

"Tell me about it," she says.

"No, you tell me. What have I done? I'd like to know."

She looks at me in disbelief. "The skit. I heard about the skit. Did you think I wouldn't find out?"

"I knew you would," I say. "I was going to tell you myself. I thought you'd see the hilarity of it. You, Mona, of all people."

"Tommy," she says. "I told you about my abortion. I trusted you. How could you think I'd find that hilarious?"

Wayne drops the needle on "Music Man" and people cover their ears, everyone, that is, except Mona and me. "It wasn't you I was making fun of. It was the frivolity of human passions. I mean, don't you see the least bit of humor in a gymnastics squad of sexually prolific females? The whole state knows over half the girls on the team have had abortions. Half the girls, Mona. You want to know something else? You're not to blame."

"Oh yeah," she says, "who is?"

"No one's to blame. People can't help doing what they do." I put my arm around her shoulders and her head shakes against my World War II paratrooper's jacket. "Me. I was only demonstrating school spirit."

"You're fucked!" she says.

"No," I tell her, "the world is fucked." I tell her it's not me, but the fucked world she sees *in* me.

"God, Tommy, I love you so," she says, and the two of us weave through the labyrinth of bodies, past Wayne on his way to the kitchen, past Le Chefski, who taps me on the shoulder as we pass through the door and says, "I hope you know what you're doing, penis head."

We pass Semen who is standing under a tree, a cup of beer in either hand. We pass kids smoking and drinking in small groups, pass the Mustang, with the mostly dried remnants of our bombs still adhering to edges of the windshield, and the shiny green corn harvester, to the stone wall behind the barn where at least two other couples are clenching. In the darkness I unbutton her letter jacket and slide my hand under her dacron skirt. "God, I've missed you," she says. "I thought you didn't want to see me again." I spring the single hook of her bra, which is a much simpler garment than the four-hook, underwired, ultrasupport bra Candice wears. "The only reason I came, I hoped you'd be here, Tommy, I hoped." *I'm a music man*, I say. I take her silver giraffe earring in my mouth, cup her breasts in my palms, then pinch and twist her nipples, which are not as tough and erect and swollen as Candice's get when she places my fingers on them, saying, *twist them gently, gently, yes, like so.*

Got gland in my hand, I say. I suck Mona's tongue, then she sucks mine, as I slip my hand under the elastic waistbands of her skirt and tights. Then Mona pulls her face away. "Tommy," she says, "we've been honest with each other. I've told you everything." I find her clit. *That's a clit, darling!* It is a about a third the size of Candice's. *I'm a man, a music.* I press it with my finger. "Wait. I've got to tell you something." I rub it gently. *Yes, like that. It's almost like a pickle, isn't it? Ribbed, look at it. Wet, touch it.* Candice is like a huge kosher dill compared to Mona. "Listen to me." *Gonna rip me.* "I let Wayne Le Chefski come inside me."

"Wayne?" I say.

"Yes," says Mona, wrapping her arms around my head. "Do you hate me?"

"When?"

"This afternoon, before the meet. I thought you hated me. I thought . . ." I keep rubbing her, and she opens her legs a little.

"A girl should experience everything," I say. Don't ever try to restrict a woman, Candice said.

"I don't love him," Mona says, taking my monstrous penis in her hands. Do unto others, Candice said, as you would have others do unto you. We rub each other gently. "Do you love me?" Mona asks. "Say you do. Say it. Say it. Say it."

"I love you, Mona," says Wayne Le Chefski. He is standing in the snow, next to the pigsty, the shotgun propped against his shoulder. "I love you," he says again, and as he does the other couples break from one another and look on from beside the barn. Kids who were outside the house gather around Wayne Le Chefski and us. "Come on," says Mike Schleuter, who is the captain of the football team, "put the gun down, Wayne." I see Semen standing next to the stone wall, both of his cups refilled with beer. From the house comes Testosterone Catastrophe, "Mary . . . I wanna, wanna, wanna eat your heart!" I kiss Mona on the ear, walk up to where Wayne Le Chefski is standing, stoic, like a statue, and plug the barrel of his shotgun with my thumb.

"Go ahead. Blow me apart, Wayne."

"Pull out your thumb!"

"Please," I say, "blow me apart!"

"Please," he says, "pull your thumb out of the barrel."

I do, and he fires, and Mona splatters against the wall of the barn. I am recounting the truth of what happened November 24, 1996, at approximately 11:15 p.m., at least insofar as words are ever capable *of recounting the truth*. Yet, the particulars of Mona's death are not what concerns me. What does, and what should concern you (if you have read this far and not just turned here by accident!) is that a group of lobbyists in Washington, D.C.—composed of parents, church leaders, and the wives of two prominent U.S. senators—called the Parents' Music Resource Center, is trying to make it impossible for kids like me to purchase audio and video recordings like the ones I have either alluded to or mentioned by name, because they believe such works of art are contributing to the corruption of our nation's youth. As a youth, I maintain such works of art are only as corrupt as the world they depict, our world, the world you and I share! In a matter of a half page, if you will bear with me, I will describe in graphic detail how the buckshot entered Mona just below her rib cage, what she said as she looked down at the shotgun hole in her black dacron blouse, how the crowd dispersed and Wayne Le Chefski and I were arrested by the police. But you must bear in mind as you read that I am only able to do so because of songs like "Sweet Surrender" by Open and Gaping, "Love Me Tender" by Sick Fuck, "(What Do You Get) When You Fall in Love" by Proud Felch, songs I have listened to hundreds of times, without whose imagery I would be left groping for words. Or worse, be forced to use frogs as a metaphor, the only creatures besides Mona I have ever seen splatter (!), one summer night each year, off car doors, bumpers, and grilles—when Semen and I have collected enough of them off the cul-de-sac to make it worth our while. Frogs barely the size of a human appendix! Is that how you would have me describe a ninth-grade girl's disembowelment and death? Clearly we must *band* together, no pun intended, and fight against the fascists who want to restrict our rights (rights granted in the Constitution of our great nation!) to appreciate the art of our choice!

WAYNE LE CHEFSKI PULLS THE TRIGGER AND FIRE FLASHES from the barrel past my right shoulder and for several long and pleasurable seconds, about thirty of us stand there in a semicircle staring at Mona, unaware that anything extraordinary has even happened. At first not even Mona is aware. She says, "Let's leave." But when she tries to pull herself from the wall and can't (because the buckshot has more or less plastered her to the stone!), that's when we see the bulge in her blouse, which is really a hole, from which an organ is attempting to spill! "Oh my god, oh my god, oh my god," says Mike Schleuter. Two or three kids scream. Some scramble back to the house, some to their cars. A couple of boys put their arms under Wayne Le Chefski's shoulders and help him away over the snow a step at a time. In the midst of the excitement, I walk over to Mona, whose thin nyloned legs prop the rest of her body against the side of the barn like the stand of an easel.

"Look," she says when I am standing before her, "I'm giving birth."

"No, you're not," I tell her.

I help her with the buttons of her blouse, help her pull the tattered dacron away from the edges of the hole and from what looks like a shiny blue head. "Feel," she says and places both of my palms on the soft, hairless scalp. "Is it a boy or a girl?"

"I don't think it has eyes, a nose, or mouth."

"I don't care," she says, "I love it anyway," and as her shoulders begin to shake, I feel her baby's head jiggle and turn of its own accord. "It's coming," she says. "Help it come, Tommy."

I place my hands on either side of its soft head, where it should have had ears, and feel its thin neck between my fingers. "Pull, Tommy." I pull, but it won't come, so I reach in and take its warm entangled body in my hands.

"I don't think it has any arms," I say.

"I don't care. It's ours, Tommy. It's ours." As I pull, its body unravels into long fleshy tubing, which I raise in my fists and show to Mona. "That's its umbilical cord, stupid." I feel our baby breathe and cry. "You have to cut that, Tommy. Do you have a knife? Find someone with a knife. You have to cut it or it'll die!"

I look for someone with a knife and see Semen doubled over by the corner of the barn, spilling beer onto the snow from his mouth. "You all right?" I ask him.

He shakes his head.

"You have to cut it!" Mona cries.

"You have a knife, Semen? A pocket knife or something?"

"Can't you bite it off?" Mona asks. I let go of the glistening blue head, and it hangs outside her blouse by a second neck, which curls upward into the hole. I take a step backward as more and more of its "umbilical cord" unravels through the opening, coiling onto the snow between her shoes. I kneel in the warmth, put my mouth to the hard juncture, and sink my teeth into the fibrous tubing. There are sirens, red and blue flashing lights. Mona tries to cradle the baby, but its second neck prevents her from lifting it very high. My face is covered with warmth. The tissue snaps, a granular, black liquid spews from the severed end of the hose onto my face, onto my white World War II paratrooper's jacket, as Mona pulls the baby free.

"There," I say. I hear a long loud cry like the wail of a newborn baby, but it is only Semen who has watched Mona pull her own stomach out of the hole and rock it in her arms. Five police officers round the corner of the barn. Two of them pull me away from Mona, twist my arms behind my back, force my face into the cold stone. They tell me anything I say can and will be used against me. "I've got nothing to hide," I tell them. They slam my head into the wall. I tell them it's nobody's fault! I tell them I can explain everything! that Mr. Morrel signed the form! he didn't know what was in the skit, but he signed the form anyway! my mother made me irresistible to women! she showed me how to touch them! how to make them peal with rapture! my father was no good with women! my mother told me how he'd just lie there after he shot his load in her! how he'd go to sleep like a fish! Mona wanted a baby so much it affected her mind! her parents were mean! her mother put her hand on the burner when she was just a little girl! her father touched her places she didn't want to be touched! Mona told me so many times! but then, they can't help it if their own parents raised them that way! their lives are hard, too! Wayne Le Chefski only wanted a girlfriend! Mona only wanted love and affection! Mr. Morrel's so overworked! he only wanted a nap! Milty and Ak don't want to lose the glory that once was theirs as fighting men of our great nation! don't make them move into Harris Machinery! my mother has my best interest at heart! she doesn't want me to grow up to be a loser with women! Mr. Morrel only wants our girls to do well on the balance beam, floor, and mat! Wayne Le Chefski's parents have got enough to do feeding the hogs and milking the cows without worrying themselves over two wild and reckless sons! even Harold W. Lindstrom, M.D., is trying to be a good second husband for Candice! even if he's married to someone else! he can't help that! why just last week he gave me twenty dollars from his wallet! twenty dollars without which I'd have had to wait to buy the new Pus CD!

"Shut up!" says Wayne Le Chefski. He is sitting next to me in the back of the patrol car. "They can't hear a word you're saying! They've got us in the cage."

I try to grip the wire screen that separates the front and back seats, but my wrists are restricted by cuffs. On the other side of it is an inch-thick pain of soundproof glass, through which I see the two police officers smoking pipes. As we move toward town, they draw the smoke through the stems in unison, and it leaves their mouths in tiny crests which swirl before the lit-up dash, thickening the haze in which they work.

ZERO

EXCEPT ON TUESDAYS, WHEN ZERO HIMSELF SITS DOWN AT his baby grand and tinkles out showtunes for a crowd of year-rounders, his establishment empties out in the winter by ten o'clock. I know because I've waitressed and tended bar here off and on since I came to Provincetown seventeen years ago, "in the motherly way," as they say, at twenty-three and married to a sexually confused painter named Thaw Stuyvesant. Truthfully speaking, there isn't a restaurant in this town that could have seen me through to where I am today, the tediousness of which no one but a paid professional should have to listen to and, believe me, has. But I'm tired by the time the last customers on a blustery Wednesday night in February square their bills with me. The wood is wiped, the salts and peppers topped, the ketchups straightened and the coffeepots emptied. I'm ready to watch the Letterman Show with my son Chris, who in seven months goes to Dennison University in Granville, Ohio, which might as well be Alaska for how often I'll see him, when the sound of piano keys drifts across the dining room, a riff from "If

He Walked into My Life," written by Jerry Herman for the musical *Mame*.

"Shell," Zero croons in the half-light, "come sit with me on the bench. I want you to sing Angela Lansbury's part."

"Tuesday was yesterday and next Tuesday's still six days away," I call to him from the bar where I'm balancing the cash register. "Anyhow, you usually sing Mame's part." The cook has left, the prep boy, too.

"Aw, Shel-*lee*," he says and adds just enough discord to the melody to make me lose my count of the dimes.

The restaurant has more stained glass in its windows than many churches do, and through a depiction of the crucifixion I see snow falling outside, clumps the size of cotton balls casting shadows on Christ's tendinous legs and arms and lilting head. Zero sits with his back to me, a sad, fat queen whose silk pullovers cling to his belly and breasts. There is nothing I wouldn't do for this man, I've told myself at times when the miraculousness of just being alive swelled inside me. But tonight isn't one of them.

"I'm sorry, Zero. I'm tired. I'm going home to pop some popcorn and curl up in front of the television with Chris."

"Drew's dead," Zero says, lifting his hands from the keys as if they're claws. Against the shiny black of the piano's propped lid, Zero's silver goatee and mustache, which a hair stylist trims once a week, are sharp accouterments to an otherwise drained and flaccid profile. All of us working at the restaurant have expected the news, for Drew has been in bed upstairs for almost two years. I leave the coins uncounted on the bar, cross a room decorated with *objets d'art* that Zero has spent his life collecting: a painted wooden horse from a Coney Island carousel, a carving of Inuit Eskimos skinning a seal, a replica of a winged gargoyle from the cathedral at Nôtre Dame, as well as a Thaw Stuyvesant beach scene. I rest my hand on his shoulder.

"When did it happen?" I ask.

"At precisely eight thirty-nine," Zero replies.

"Where is he?" I ask, and Zero lifts his eyes, which would mean something different if Zero believed in an afterlife, but he doesn't. "Would you like me to call someone?" I ask, though the nearest funeral home, twenty minutes away in good weather, isn't going to send a man into the blizzard.

"No, no. I want to leave Drew right where he is for the night." On top of the piano, on either side of the sheet music, stand two martinis, a plump green olive swimming elegantly in each. I reach for the one Zero has made for me, but think better of it and retract my hand. "Oh, don't be a scared-ee pants," he says. "Please. Drink."

"Just this one," I say, though I have never in my life drunk just one.

We clink rims and Zero says, "Let's get tight, like we used to, back when your life was a mess and you were much more fun. For Drew's sake."

In truth I never liked Drew, a handsome, untalented actor whose vanity prevented his seeing any point of view but his own, but Zero's criticism snags. *I have become a bore*, I think. "I'll sing the Georgia millionaire suitor's part," I say. "You sing the impoverished, bedraggled Mame's."

"You're an angel, darling, an angel with invisible wings." Zero slugs his martini, olive and all, and strains another into his glass from a stainless steel martini shaker he's concealed behind the music desk. Setting his glass back on the piano, his hand quivers the way mine used to after a day on the wagon, and I wonder if he's hidden a drinking problem all these years, when his elbows strike the keys in a cacophony of sharps and flats. I pull him close, and his flesh jiggles against me like a pudding's firm crust. "I'm sorry," he says, wiping his eyes. "I am."

"Don't be," I say. At sixty-three Zero is a respected owner of downtown real estate. His vast holdings include the comfortable, waterview apartment above Mason's Saltwater Taffy that my son and I have shared his entire life, and yet Zero is so like a child that even I, who know better, have sometimes underestimated his formidable business sense. He came here years before the town became a haven for gays and lesbians, before he even knew he was homosexual, and in the depressed market of the late 60s bought up property that would make him a millionaire by the beginning of a heyday talked about, by those who remember it, as if it is already myth. I can barely recall it, a five year period at most, when the bright, collegiate middle of the late 70s and early 80s fashion spectrum wafted like proudly-worn flags. From the east end of Commercial Street to the west, designer T-shirts and V-neck sweaters. Every fag a flag! Autonomy proclaimed in conforming to close shaves and Polo by Ralph Lauren.

I speak of the men, for they were the ones who revivified the town, who opened bookstores and boutiques with streamers, cake, and champagne punch, and when the pandemic descended first as a rumor, not to be heeded, then as an all-out assault of nature, they formed a defensive front, threw fashion shows in which the models, gorgeous one and all, were transvestites, transsexuals, and those caught somewhere in between—drag balls, talent contests, afternoon tea dances and all-night raves, each event a carefully staged fund-raiser. At the center of the whirlwind sat Zero, the mastermind, as overweight then as now, telephoning directives with the same limitless energy with which he collected art and surrounded himself with devotees like my ex, Thaw, and, later, me.

I rub Zero's back. "You did everything you could for Drew." It's all I can think of to comfort him, for as much as I care about him, as much as I need to be here with him now, I'm preoccupied with David Letterman's guest list, wondering who I'll miss.

"There are those," Zero says, "who will be glad to learn of Drew's death. Elated even. They won't be proud of the emotion, but they'll be feeling it."

"Drew wasn't a nice person. He treated you like he treated a lot of people. Badly."

"He treated me according to his nature," Zero replies, "which was neither good nor bad."

"Anyway," I say, "I doubt anyone will be elated. Relieved maybe, after what Drew put you through, when he was sick and before, but the people we're talking about, Zero, are your friends. They care about you."

"My friends," he says, "my grand and glorious friends," and as his fingers flutter over the keys I think he will break into song. But he doesn't. "Do you know what they'll do when they hear the news?" he asks. "Do you? They'll gather around me like hungry gulls, each vying for a peck at the remains. Oh, they'll be sweet and weepy, but their tears will be corrupt. In each will be a speck of blood, like that within an egg. Which is how the spirit slips, drip by telling drip, from shells it finds uninhabitable."

"Zero," I say, "snap out of it," feeling less irritated by his self-involvement than I *ought* to be. "It doesn't become you."

"What doesn't become me? My grief, or that I see my fine friends for who they are?"

"*Remains*," I say as if I'm correcting his grammar, "are what the dead leave behind. You aren't dead, far from it, and if you think morbidity will bring you sympathy, you're sadly mistaken."

"Huh," he says as if my tone has betrayed the very disingenu-ousness he's seen in others, and perhaps it does, for I'm tired; it's been a long day with few customers, and I want to go home. "You assume I have it in me to love again. Well, I've shot my wad. Shot it once and for all."

There is stubbornness in his voice, and as I wag my head I can't help imagining Chris checking the clock above the television, not believing till he sees me that I will actually return, for at a period in my life, I may as well admit it, I set precedents I will never be able to erase entirely from his memory. "Give me an F," I tell Zero, this being the key we naturally sing in.

Zero gulps what's left of his martini, this from a man who has tried, in vain, to teach me to savor a single well-made cocktail. "Do you want to sing or no?" I ask him.

"No," he says, and anger wells within me. "Take off your jacket, my dear," he says, and my winter parka drops from my shoulders and rests on the floor as sturdily as the suit of mail propped in a corner below Christ's stigmatized feet. With its tarnished visor pulled back to a wretched, ungainly plume, the iron knight sits with a perpetual grin, the butt of many a waiter's joke, for its tubular codpiece seems to protect a prodigious erection. But it is the gaping smile, the smug, dark crescent in the hollow head, that transfixes me now.

"I would like you to accompany me upstairs." Zero rises to his polished patent leathers, his legs trunk-like from bearing so much weight. "I would like us to gaze upon the dead." He reaches for his cane.

"Zero, no," I say. "I can't. Won't."

"Won't?" he asks.

When my mother died in an automobile accident in Falmouth, my father handled the details of her cremation. When my father died twelve months later of a bleeding ulcer, I handled the details of his from sixty miles away because I was afraid of seeing his body. "I've never seen a corpse before," I tell him, "and if I went through the rest of my life without seeing one, I'd be happy."

"No, you wouldn't," he says and ambles toward a spiral staircase that punctures the second story like a drill bit. In the mid-70s the upstairs served as a discotheque. When disco died, Zero put a waterbed in the center of the parquet dance floor and brought his lovers there, often during the supper hour, sometimes two, three, or more at once, turning off all the lights but the gel spots, which splintered off a mirror ball into swirling myriads of greens, yellows, and blues. I remember waiting tables in the restaurant when the ceiling pulsed with each heaving swish of Zero's bed, looking up through the circular passageway and wondering if Zero was giving or receiving. With the right partner, he could have been either. But years have passed since then, and the thin gold chain that hung between the balustrades with the warning, *EMPLOYEES ONLY*, dangles from a single railing that Zero grips as he hefts his legs up the blond oak risers.

"Lock the door when you leave." He speaks without facing me, his bulging ass and thighs suspended above the floor like a trawler's catch. "And leave your key on the bar."

"So this is what it finally comes to. Firing me because I won't go upstairs."

"Interpret my words however you like, my dear," he says and continues his ascension at a donkey's pace.

"Fine."

I pick up my parka from the floor and chug the rest of my martini. I remove the restaurant key from my key chain and leave it on the bar next to my martini glass. Tonight, I'll be home in time to catch "Stupid Human Tricks," Chris's favorite Late Show routine, and, like half our winter population, collect unemployment until Memorial Day.

"And Shell," Zero calls from above, "your eviction notice will arrive at your address by the end of the week. I simply ask that you be respectful of the terms as they are outlined in our lease agreement."

"My what?" I want to give him the opportunity to retract this blow.

"On the apartment, my dear."

It's an unwritten rule in this town that no one, however delinquent they are with rent, is turned out in winter, and I've sent my checks to Zero on time for seventeen years. "I think what you're doing is cheap and manipulative! I've worked hard for you. I've done you no wrong. In fact, I'm devoted to you." The ceiling creaks as he walks across it. "You hear me, Zero?" But there is only the wind and the rattling of stained glass.

"All right," I say. "You win. I'm coming up." I reach the landing in a third the time it took Zero, who is sitting behind his mahogany desk. It's at an angle from the deceased more befitting a psychiatrist than a primary caregiver, though the room itself, with its walls of rough-hewn lumber and black paint, looks more like the office of a small-time racketeer. On nightstands on either side of the bed flicker beeswax candles, like those that line the bar. With no windows and little ventilation, the air is stagnant and I'm seeing stars which, as Zero beckons me to him with his hand, I realize are the flames, replicated into slowly shifting galaxies by the mirror ball.

A smile passes over Zero's face, which reflects off the glistening desktop. "You have no idea, my dear, of the toil endured by the homosexual man," he says. "But the fault's not yours. Some women have had an innate understanding of what I'm talking about—Davis, Garbo, Dietrich all had it, and Monroe might have, had she lived long enough to show it—but most, I'm afraid, do not."

Behind me lies the dead. "Sit, please," Zero says, though there is nowhere to sit but on the bed. "The dead must make room for the living," he says. "Isn't that your credo?" I touch the Naugahyde frame with my fingers. As I sit on it, liquid gives way along the edge of the mattress and ripples out beneath the dead. For a moment I believe Drew is shifting toward me. "Most women," Zero continues, "possess a far more acute sense of the interconnectedness of things than most men. It's what makes them better child-rearers, this dogged faith in the process over the end result, in continuation, circularity, and the unfathomable logic of change."

"Isn't it possible," I ask, "that women acquired such instincts from being cast into maternal roles since time immemorial, and that if men—"

"I'm not talking about the how and why of it," Zero cuts in, "but about the *is* of it."

Animated by candlelight, his features take on a ghoulish look. "Do you even know who you're talking to?" I want to ask, but his eyes have glassed over, and in their reflection must lurk the friend he knows I am.

"When a man fucks another man," he says calmly, "his nihilism is complete, tangible, there for him to taste and smell and squeeze. The act itself, even in cases involving real feeling, cannot be the progenerative act heterosexuals know it to be, even as they preclude the question of offspring with so many precautionary measures. To possess such potency, my dear, to have to gird oneself with prophylactics, spermicides, and pills, not to protect oneself, but to protect such a gift of oneself, is a pleasure the gay man will never know. Sex between fags is quintessentially a squandering of seed, for as feminine or as masculine as a fairy may be, his repository is the colon, the mouth, the hand."

"I know all about nihilism," I say.

When, no longer the least confused, Thaw Stuyvesant left me for a man, a boy really, nineteen, with less hair on his body than a fish, I spent seven years numbing myself with alcohol and prescription pain-killers. If I met a reasonably good-looking, straight man at a bar, I went home with him, passed out mid-fuck, and learned in the morning of his criminal record. Mutual friends of ours who stuck with me after Thaw and his boytoy left town were gay, anyone the least bit interesting was gay, and in an atmosphere of liberation reminiscent of the 70s singles scene I managed to avoid the squalor of my soiled sheets by looking forward to the intoxicated free-for-all each evening held in store. Aided by my gay friends, I gauged potential sex partners by their physiques alone and at Happy Hour held up my end of conversations with the details of my sexual exploits. *Ah honey, if only you were a man . . .* When I was drunk, or if I was high, the nihilism of my ways shimmered like sateen and halos hovered about the heads of my cohorts. As, one by one, my friends took to their beds for weeks at a stretch, it was as if our lifestyle was acquiring a patina, and we clung to our profligacy as if it were bronze, all the more valuable for showing its age. Not until they began to drop from sight, and I would read their obituaries in the local paper, did I think to reexamine my life. When I did I saw Chris, ten.

"I don't think you do," Zero says. "If you did, you'd have more compassion for Drew, lying behind you, dead."

"That's just it, he's dead," I say. "You and me, we're survivors. When the net was dropped, it missed us somehow. Or maybe it didn't, but we're alive now, and others are, too, and they deserve our compassion. Not the dead."

"I admire the sentiment," Zero says. "I've felt it myself from time to time." He stands, and as reflections of candlelight pass across his face, his black silk pullover, his huge hands, he says, "I'm going to concoct another round of martinis, and then I'm going to tell you something that's very difficult for me."

Zero shuffles across the dance floor to a bar I haven't seen since it was peopled five thick and tended by bare-chested bodybuilders in bowties. He pours gin into a shaker of ice, makes a drink I've made thousands of. "My dear," he says as he holds out an isosceles triangle of my poison, "I must let you go. I've no choice in the matter really. I've liquidated my assets and nothing's left."

I take the martini, and Zero carries his around the desk to the bed. "You had to cover Drew's medical bills," I say, doing my best to sound sympathetic, and Zero laughs.

"If modern medicine were all Drew required," he places a hand on my head, "I could've kept him alive till he became a very old faggot indeed. But he wanted to be rich before he died, so I put a fortune at his fingertips and made him happier in sickness than he ever was in health."

Zero's thigh brushes my shoulder, and from his crotch wafts a sweet but overpowering *eau de Cologne*. "You gave him everything?" I ask.

"I gave him a line of credit equaling my net worth," Zero says, "and he succeeded in spending it in under two years. Something of a record, wouldn't you say? He accomplished it with the red telephone I installed beside his bed."

I crane my neck to see this telephone and find myself looking into Drew's face. This is the only corpse I've ever seen, and as I take in Drew's wan lids and wasted cheeks and the perfectly relaxed state of each muscle, I feel none of the fear I thought, fear not of death or the unknown, but of the gladness I might have felt, even had it been but a modicum, at the death of someone I competed with for Zero's affection. In productions Zero funded, Drew was worse than bad, barking lines written by Williams, O'Neill, and Pinter as if each bore the same emotional weight. In his ability to sniff from people how much to the cent they were willing to part with, I saw the bloodhound in him revealed again. That he wanted nothing to do with me I took as further proof of his acumen, for I was never in a position to part with anything. As I stand to get the full view, there is a swish, the waterbed bolsters back, and for a moment it's as if we're watching Drew float out to sea, his pillowed head and blanketed lower parts rocking almost imperceptibly as about us the galaxies swirl.

"He sent cars to his sisters," Zero says, "and explained Kant to phone sex operators." He sighs. "I'd hoped to put Chris through college. Indeed, I'd hoped to do a lot of things."

"That's what you wanted to tell me?"

Zero clears his throat. "I'm no longer in a position to shave off the sharp edges for people. I'm done, finished." As he speaks, he sounds relieved. With two martinis down, I wrap my arms around him. "You're not angry at me?" he asks.

How can I answer this, when without his support I might have perished long ago? "I'm eternally indebted to you," I tell him. "I'm your number one fag hag."

Zero laughs. "Then will you sing with me now? Downstairs? At the piano?"

"No," I tell him. "I'm going home." And I leave him there.

WHEN I REACH MASON'S SALTWATER TAFFY, CHRIS IS WATCHING television on the second story of the old yellow house we've rented for years, the screen colorful and warm, flickering on the walls and glass, only I do not know how to tell him I can no longer afford his schooling or a lot of things we have learned to take for granted. Inside the darkened storefront, the stainless steel arms of an industrial taffy mixer curve around the lip of a fifty-gallon mixing bowl. Reflected in the pane I see a portrait of myself in my parka. I walk past boarded-up storefronts to the Governor Bradford, the only drinking establishment open at this time of night, at this time of year, and though friends are playing chess just inside the doors, I continue onto the wharf.

It's lit, from the shoreline out over the water to where a fleet of dilapidated fishing boats rock gently against one another, connected by ropes. I look at the rusty hulls—if one boat were to sink, would it drag the others down, too?—and turn to wonder at the lights in town.